R.B. ROUGE

Tobacco-Stained Prayers

First published by VJK Publishing 2025

Publisher:

VJK Publishing

USA, Louisiana
United States of America
First edition
ISBN(paperback):979-8-9999117-0-4

Cover art by A. Ancona

DEDICATION

For my parents:— Whose love made me tough as a rock, crazy Af, and loss shaped me forever.

This book is for you both. Proof love can raise the dead and keep the lost from staying lost.

Mama- Mrs. B — (1956-2017)

Daddy- Kimbo— (1956–1991)

“When trauma is your inheritance, better be real careful how you spend it.

R. B. Rouge

Contents

Foreword

"When madness runs in the blood, you learn to build altars out of whatevers left."

This book is a work of fiction, set in altered towns with names changed—some to protect the innocent, some to protect the guilty, and some left untouched for nostalgia's sake. But make no mistake—fiction can still bleed when it's cut from real wounds.

It only takes three generations to train a free people into forgetting their chains. I've seen the proof of that in my own bloodline.

I call this story *Tobacco-Stained Prayers.* It's fictional, but it has a pulse. If you want to know the story behind the story—how a painting foretold a birth, how ink and blood collided—☞ Visit →patreon.com/rb_rouge

They say some stories are written in blood. Mine? It was painted in it.

Painting: Born to Fail *by A. Ancona — Featured in* Born to fail *(2005) by Rena Bergeron / R.B. Rouge.— a prophecy written in oil, sealed in blood memory.*

"The sins of the fathers shall be visited upon the children unto the third and fourth generation." — Exodus 20:5

Preface

I didn't plan to write this book. Some stories don't ask permission—they pull you back whether you want them to or not. This is fiction, built on the bones of real places, hard lessons, and scars that speak even when you don't. Names are changed. Events bent. The truth filtered through a storyteller's lens—because sometimes that's the only way it can be told.

This is the first part of a larger story. When trauma is your inheritance, you'd better be real careful how you spend it.

If you're looking for something pretty, this isn't it. This is the kind of story that leaves a mark.

—R.B. Rouge

Acknowledgments

To my babies — the ones I birthed and the ones God slid into my life like secret blessings. You've each got a piece of me, whether you call me Mama, Maw maw, or Bonus-Mama.

Orand III, Taylor, & Tahj — my originals, the first heartbeat of my crew, the ones who watched me fall, rise, wobble, and reroute without ever pulling their love off the table. Y'all are the blueprint, the reason I sharpen my pen and my purpose.

Leighton, Orand IV, Aurelia, Bjorn, & Krew — my wild-hearted grands.

C.J., Lexi,Saxon, Claire, Caroline, Kimmy, Caden, Niya, Alisha, Cohen, and Autumn — my ride-or-die bonus babies:

Y'all are the thunder in my chest and the sparkle in every crazy dream I chase. Each of you carries a whole universe in your eyes, and watching your little worlds grow keeps mine spinning in the right direction. You're my chaos, my comedy, my compass, and the reason I keep turning every scar into a story worth handing down.

This ain't a diary. This is a story. A damn good one. And it marks my return — to the page, to the grind, to the art of making something outta everything.

Special Thanks To:

To Chris F — the real one in the room. For showing up, standing tall, and holding the line when the world wobbled. Your presence hit different, and this book carries a little of your backbone in its spine.

And to Steven E., my mentor, my financer, my sponsor, my chauffeur, my bodyguard — the giant who stood shoulder-to-shoulder with my chaos and never blinked. This book made it to daylight because you did.

And to A. Ancona — your art has walked beside my words for over twenty years. Thank you for your support, your vision, and for letting your work live a second life on this cover.

To everyone who ever offered me a second, third, or maybe even fourth chance—thank you.

And to anyone reading this who's carrying too much hurt and too many regrets: you are not too far gone. Tell your story. Let it go. Leave something honorable behind.

And remember—if you woke up today, you don't have to do anything, but you get to.

That's already a one-up… at least on the dead.

With gratitude and swamp-born stubbornness,

—R.B. Rouge

[illegible] — you've walked beside me [illegible] for over twenty years. Thank you for your support, your vision, and for all the hard work [illegible].

To everyone who ever offered me a second [illegible] or maybe even [illegible] a chance [illegible].

And to anyone reading this who's carrying too much hurt and too many regrets: you are not too far gone [illegible] honorable [illegible].

And remember [illegible] you don't have to do anything, but you [illegible].

[illegible]

[illegible]

Introduction

Author's Reckoning

Hey podna, lean in. This ain't no soft sermon wrapped in lace. If you came lookin' for comfort, you best turn your truck around and keep drivin'. What you're holdin' is a blood-soaked ledger—**Tobacco-Stained Prayers**—and it don't flinch. It's the blue pill—the descent into silence, memory, and myth. The second book, *Saltwater Knuckles*, is the red—where mercy tastes like blood and memory fights back.

Down here on the bayou, trauma ain't just inherited—it's bartered, buried, and baptized. We don't pass down heirlooms; we pass down silence, and silence cuts deeper than any blade. This book is fiction, sure—but it's stitched from real bones and whispered truths. We tell it slant because straight talk gets you buried or branded. But don't mistake the slant for softness. This story pulses. It bruises. It remembers.

This ain't a diary. It's a reckoning. A holy one. Built from the kind of family you survive by storytelling—where myth is memory's armor and laughter is a weapon against the dark. I speak for the bloodline-bound and the code-breakers, the ones who learned to love through locked doors and sideways glances.

You'll meet Maw Sunny, who could bless or blister with the same breath, and a Daddy who came back from the service cracked open, swearing he was a Frizbitarian who landed on God's roof. You'll walk the thin line between madness and manipulation, where copper-tasting water and confession share the same faucet.

We don't name our feelings—we drown them, fight them, or vanish beneath them. And when you start asking what's yours and what was programmed to keep you quiet, you'll understand why this story had to be told.

This book carries the weight of domestic violence, addiction, and mental unraveling. It's the first part of a larger gospel—one that drags you back whether you want it or not. Because broken lives aren't just marked by tragedy. They're defined by the strange mercy that lingers—like tobacco-stained prayers whispered in the dark, when you thought no one was listening.

Some stories are written in blood. Mine was painted in it.

Welcome to the mess. The truth still costs too damn much.

A Word of Prophecy

"The sins of the fathers shall be visited upon the children unto the third and fourth generation."

We've lived that scripture in our marrow. I couldn't fix what came before. But I wrote it down, so the next ones don't have to guess.

1

The End Justifies The Means

I was only five when it happened.

The kind of thing a kid shouldn't carry, but somehow does—tucked deep behind the eyes where no one really dared to look.

Maybe that's when it all started.

Not the screaming, or the scars, or the silence that followed, but that quiet war inside me.

Between wanting to be loved and learning it might come with a cost.

I was a chatterbox back then.

Couldn't shut me up for shit.

Mama liked the quiet—said noise made her head hurt.

She only liked a little soft rock in the morning while she did her hair for work.

But there I was, hanging on her robe, going on and on like a broken record:

Why does Dad call you Two Tits?

Where do dreams go when you wake up?

Can I marry Freddy Krueger[1] if he says yeah?

If you die on the toilet, do you go to heaven with your pants down?

Why is your nose hair gray but your head hair is brown?

Is God a boy or a girl or a cloud with eyes?

Are aliens really demons?

Are there birthday cakes in hell, Mama, or just burnt cookies?

I'd follow her around like a lost puppy, yammering away, until she'd spin on me with that glare and hiss,

"For Lord's sake! Hush it up, Dingbat, you're driving me insane."

Half the time she meant it, but sometimes she'd laugh when she thought I wasn't looking.

I wanted to believe her laughter meant she loved me,

that maybe my questions weren't so stupid after all.

But the way she turned away, the way her eyes flicked past me like I wasn't even there—

it made me wonder if I was just noise to her.

I'd keep talking, louder and faster, trying to fill the silence,

trying to make her see me.

But the ache in my chest grew heavier every time she told me to hush.

I didn't know it then, but I was already learning how to measure love

by how much I could endure to earn it.

And if I couldn't find it here,

I'd find it somewhere else—

even if it meant breaking the rules.

I was a tomboy with a crooked bowl cut,

and this natural blonde stripe in my bangs that made people ask if Mama frosted it.

I didn't know what that meant, so I just told them "prolly,"

thinking it was something cool moms did at slumber parties with their daughters.

I wished my mom was cool,

but that's okay—Maw Sunny, she was cool enough for both of 'em.

I spent most of my time with Maw Sunny—my grandma, Mama's mama.

Me and Mama lived at her house.

Maw Sunny didn't mind noise as long as it was her kind of noise.
She'd take me fishing before the sun even got up,
and every now and then she'd let me have a pony of my own—
a tiny beer she sipped on all day.
I didn't know it was beer.
I just heard folks ask her, "Sonny, you got any ponies left?"
and I thought they meant My Little Pony.
I'd ask her,
"What color is it?
Can I braid its mane?
Does it have sparkles?"
She'd just give me that look over her cigarette like,
Lord, help this child.
I was probably three the first time I set foot in a bar.
Maw used to bring me to The Rusty Rougarou down the road.
She had a girlfriend who worked there.
"Now when we go in, you ask the barmaid for a Shirley Temple like you grown."
Boy, I thought I was fancy.
Nobody else in there, just us, early in the day while Maw made her rounds.
"Maw, can I have some quarters for the bull?"
I'd spring everything that could be sprung,
trying to hold on to that old rusted mechanical bull.
Most days I played hairstylist on my dolls,
but I did not do no beauty-queen bullshit.
Barbie and Stacy were lame.
I wanted them to look like Cyndi Lauper[2] or Boy George[3]—
blue streaks, shaved sides, eyeliner for days.
I don't know how many times my mama threatened to hang me from the ceiling fan
and beat my ass like a piñata for ruining their hair.
"That doll cost good money!" she'd holler at me.
I wasn't allowed to play with the other kids either.

Maw Sunny said they carry trouble like fleas.
So it was just me on the porch,
talking to my lineup of decapitated Barbies and invisible children.
I wondered what it would be like to have friends of my own.
The only kids I ever really got to play with
were my two cousins, Jasmine and Buzz,
every other weekend when I visited at Daddy's.
I remember wishing I had a sibling to play with
or even just one real friend.
They were in Cub Scouts and Brownies.
They had a mama and a daddy that lived together.
They had each other.
So naturally, one summer afternoon,
I was swinging barefoot in the yard,
watching Maw through the kitchen window
when I saw 'em.
Kids on bikes—Matt, Jenny, Aaron, Chris, Dana.
They slowed, eyed the fence, and hollered for me.
My heart exploded in my chest.
I wasn't supposed to.
I knew I wasn't supposed to.
But gosh, I couldn't help it.
"I ride bikes too, kids!
Kids!
Hey, kids, you wanna come play with me?"
All the while looking back in paranoia.
"Come in," I whispered,
leading them through the gate behind the house.
For the first time in my five years on this earth,
I belonged.
We played hide and seek, tag, laughed so hard my stomach hurt.
But magic… it never stays.
It shifts.

Vanishes.
And when it breaks,
it doesn't leave a crack—
it leaves a crater.
We collapsed in the grass, sweaty and smiling.
"Hey," Chris said,
"can you get us something to drink?"
I hesitated.
My belly flipped.
But I wanted them to stay.
"Okay. I'll see what we got."
I crept into the kitchen.
"Maw, can I have some drinks for my friends?
We're thirsty."
She spun, spatula in hand.
"Who is we?
You know I don't want those ugly ass inbred children trampling my lawn."
"But they're nice—"
"I'll fix you something.
But you tell those filthy little shits to go on home.
Ain't got no damn business being over here trying to ruint you."
She handed me a glass of sweet tea.
My hand trembled.
It spilled all up on my shirt.
Outside, I mumbled,
"Sorry, we don't have nothing right now."
Dana's eyes went cold.
"That's okay. We were gonna play a different game anyway."
I perked up.
"Okay. What game?"
"Ever played doctor?"
Dana grabbed my arm.
And just like that,

the day bent in a way I couldn't straighten back out.
Maw Sunny came storming out the door,
apron still dusted in flour,
hollering at the kids to get on home.
"That's enough playin' out here—git before I snatch ya bald-headed!"
she barked, broom raised like a switch.
The kids scattered,
but her eyes weren't on them.
They were on me—
sharp and knowing,
like she'd caught a whiff of something foul
that didn't belong in her yard.
Afterward, I curled up on the couch beside her.
The Muppets were on—
Maw called them the mop-heads.
They were cooking something on TV—
one of them stirring a big pot of soup.
Right as the Muppet leaned in and sniffed the steam, saying,
"Doesn't that smell delicious?"
Maw Sonny let out the biggest, stinkiest beer fart I'd ever heard in my life.
I gagged and yelled,
"That don't smell very delicious to me, Maw!"
She cackled so hard she nearly fell off the couch.
That moment broke the silence,
but the ache stayed.

Sonny May was a sharp old gal from north Louisiana.
Just because she played stupid didn't mean she was.
I tried my best to keep Mama from finding out,

but she sure as shit she did.
When Mama came home from her night class,
she was all work—hair
up-do with that twenty-four-hour lipstick smile on.
But she could still sniff out trouble like a bloodhound.
She hadn't even pulled the key from the ignition
when our ol' flip-flop-faced neighbor hollered from across the yard,
"Your mama scared those kids off today!"
Mama gave her that tight-lipped, Thanks, I'll handle it smile
and turned to Maw Sunny.
"What the hell is that woman yelling about?
You running off some kids?"
I tried to fake sleep, but it was useless.
Next thing I know,
she's shaking my shoulder.
"Ramey, wake your ass up."
She handed me Gizmo and Spike,
my new Gremlin[4] figurines from my birthday.
"I know those kids did something to you," she said,
voice low.
"It's okay.
Show me what.
Your toys."
I stared at her.
Is this a trick question?
Even then, I was too embarrassed to tell the truth.
She snatched those toys.
"Was it like this?"
Smash!
"Or like this?"
"We played tag," I mumbled.
"Uh huh.
Tag, you say?"

She beat the bricks off my ass that night—
partly because I lied,
partly because I let them in,
and… well, maybe because I peed in her bed that night.
She hated that.
And I hated that shit, too.
She could rough me up if she wanted,
but she'd be damned somebody else would.
Honestly, I was good at blocking things out.
Pretty sure I had almost forgotten it even happened
until she started humping my damn toys together.
I never even thought about my toys doing that before.
But after that—
damage done.
For months, when nobody was looking,
those Gremlins were having orgies in the toy box.
Even the Care Bears got invites.
Barbie didn't stand a chance.
It got weird.

She stood there breathing hard,
then muttered,
"The ends justify the means,"
and disappeared into the dark hallway.

2

Institution Green

We lived with Maw Sunny because of Daddy's illness.

Mama never sat me down and spelled it out, but I picked it up in pieces over the years. Daddy got discharged from the Army in 1980, and he didn't come home the same. He saw things no one else could see, heard voices no one else could hear. Sometimes he got violent. Not with me—I only saw him lose it once—but shit that was enough.

Folks around here just called it the nuthouse. Haunt-Bourne Medical & Mental Sciences Campus over in Mandeville[5]— It wasn't much of a hospital—more like a cage dressed up in vomit green walls, lockin' folks away and calling it care.

They called it treatment, but Daddy called it a pause button on hell.

People said they ran lightning through his head until his jaw went slack, then pulled every tooth clean out his head. Some said it was to stop him from biting. Others whispered it was to bleed the madness out by the roots. And a few—real quiet—said Haunt-Bourne was more than a hospital, that "medical & mental sciences" meant something else entirely.

Maybe I loved Daddy so much 'cause he let me talk. Didn't shush me like Mama did—didn't send me off with a wave and a sigh. He'd just let me chat him up, even when the stuff we talked about didn't seem to make a lick of sense.

I'm glad we had those awkward-ass conversations. Glad I asked dumb questions like, "Daddy, why'd they pull all your teeth out in boot camp?"

He didn't blink.

"Well, Slick," he said, tapping his jaw, "them teeth—that's the nice part my brain lets me remember."

I laughed, but he didn't.

"They believe they were after somethin' deeper. Something you can't see on no X-ray." He leaned in, voice low like he was telling me where the treasure was buried. "Soldier syrup,[6]" he said. "That's what they called it. Fear turned liquid. Memory you can bottle. They pulled it outta me one root at a time."

Then he smiled soft, like he was trying to tuck the dark parts under the light, snatched me into a headlock, and gave me a lil brese'[7] with his knuckles.

"Don't worry, Slick," he said. "You still got all yours. Keep 'em. They hold more than you think."

My first memories of Daddy live in those sterile, institution-green rooms. They called it "***Family Day***." The smell still clings to me: disinfectant and old sorrow.

Faces blurred, voices hollow, like someone had turned the volume down on their lives. Nobody smiled. Even Daddy's eyes looked drugged, like something behind them had been switched off and rewired.

Those days felt staged, like we were actors in a play we didn't know the lines for. And sometimes, if I looked long enough, I swore I could feel the air hum—like something under the surface was taking notes.

Mama tried for a while, but she gave up. Said she wouldn't raise me around that. Maybe she couldn't handle seeing the man she married turned into a stranger. Or maybe she was scared some of it would rub off on me, or maybe she knew it would,... and just maybe that's why she was so mad all the time.

The Recorders

My earliest memories of Haunt-bourne weren't just visits. They'd separate us—Daddy one way, me another.

"It's okay, Ramey, go ahead," Mama would say, smoothing my hair before they shut the door.

I couldn't see him, but I could feel him through the walls—like his breath had settled into my bones, humming low and steady.

They'd sit me at a little metal table, tape recorder spinning, asking questions that didn't make sense on paper but somehow made my skin prickle.

"What numbers do you see?"

"What color is the lady's shirt on the other side of town?"

I didn't know how I knew. I just did. Sometimes the answers came like flashes behind my eyes, sometimes like a taste in my mouth. And when I said them out loud, the room would shift—clipboard man leaning in, mirror wall buzzing like it had ears.

They'd get excited, start asking faster, softer, like they were trying not to scare the truth off.

"Good, Ramey. What else? Can you see anything else?"

I'd squint, reach for whatever flickered next.

But it wore me out. By the time Mama picked me up, the three-hour ride back from Haunt-bourne felt like a week. My head heavy, my chest hollowed out. Like they'd scraped something from inside me and left the echo behind.

One day, I noticed something in the mirror wall—a flash of movement like someone else was behind it.

I asked, "Is there another me on the other side?"

The man with the clipboard just frowned down at me and said, "Just answer the question, sweetheart," while he patted the top of my head like I was a damn dog.

I never saw another kid in those rooms—just me, my voice on tape, and strangers behind mirrored glass.

Maw Sunny vs. Mama

Back at Maw Sunny's, life was louder, messier. She cussed like it was a second language, kept the radio hollering old jukebox hits, and never poured a drink she didn't finish. She just said what she meant, and laughed way too loud for Mama's like-in'.

But best of all—she let Daddy come over behind Mama's back. Said it was her house, her rules.

Maw Sunny was a widow with money and no patience for nonsense. She didn't need anybody, didn't chase after company, and sure as hell wasn't scared of much. If you were in her graces, you'd earned it.

I'd seen Daddy break down in her kitchen, sobbing like a boy lost in the woods. She didn't flinch. Just wrapped one long arm around his neck, popped open a pony beer, shoved it in his face and said, "Zip it up, Levi. You ain't got nothin' to cry about here. You're still my son-in-law. We're family."

And just like that, he'd quiet down. Like her words built a fence around him the world couldn't tear down.

Maw Sunny could make wringing a chicken's head clean off its neck into a whole production. While Mama was at work, she'd let me call Daddy over, and the two of them would turn the yard into a blood-sport arena—snapping necks while I stood there guessing which one would stop flopping first.

Sometimes they'd wring 'em so hard the body would take off like it had someplace urgent to be, wings flapping, legs pumping, me chasing behind with a feed bucket yelling, "You're already dead, come back!"

One time, a headless hen ran straight into the clothesline, did a backflip, and somehow landed up on the tin roof. Feathers clung to the shingles like confetti after a parade.

Daddy squinted at it, dead serious, and said, "Well, shit—that chicken was one of us."

"Daddy, what?"

He grinned, half-mad, half-holy. "I'm a Frizbitarian, you hear me? When I die, I'm gonna land on God's roof and stay there forever, just like that bird."

I froze, like maybe standing still would make the crazy pass over me. But he just kept staring at that roof, nodding, like he'd finally seen proof of his own gospel.

Looking back, Maw Sunny's the only person I've ever seen who could have a bird killed, plucked, and in the frying pan before the sun hit the tree line.

She'd serve me in bed like I was some kind of bayou princess, tray and all.

Lord, I loved fried chicken.

But I hated the smell of fresh plucked fowl—wet feathers and hot steam wrapping around my head like a dirty quilt.

Maw Sunny would just laugh and say, "Oh, stop whinin'. If that's the worst thing you ever smell, child, you'll be lucky—ha!"

Still, I pulled my weight, yanking out pinfeathers while Daddy hid behind the shed smoking a joint.

Mama was perfect. Not just pretty—precise. Hair sculpted, nails gleaming, voice soft and sweet when folks were watching. But perfect was a mask, and the drinking peeled it off in one hard pull. No warning. Just a shift in the air, and then you braced yourself.

One second I was "angel baby," the next I was getting knocked sideways because I left a cup on the wrong counter. And then she'd cry, say she was sorry, call me baby girl like nothing ever happened.

People loved her. At church they'd stop her, compliment her dress, praise how put-together she was. I used to wonder what they'd say if they ever heard how those rings sounded when she popped me upside my head.

Maw Sunny didn't try to fix Mama either. I think she was afraid of her. She'd just mutter, "Some folks care too much about looking right, not being right," then turn up the radio and ladle me gumbo like it could patch every bruise I didn't talk about.

Sometimes I'd sit between them, not sure which version of love was supposed to feel more like home.

The Quiet Thing in Me

Even then, I knew there was something different about me. At night, I'd wake up knowing things—like who was about to call, or where Maw Sunny's missing lighter was hiding, or when it was going to rain before the clouds even showed.

Maybe it was just instinct—or maybe it was whatever hum lived in the walls at Haunt-bourne, finding its way into me.

I used to think it was just kid stuff—those flashes in my head, the way I'd blurt things out without knowing why.

Mama said she used to see all kinds of things too, before I was born. Said I must've taken it from her. Said I was the only baby she ever heard of that stayed in the womb ten months. A whole month overdue.

Daddy used to call her a fat matou[8], said her face got so swollen she looked like she'd been stung by bees and blessed by the moon.

I figured I was stalling—waiting to be born under the right sign. Queen of the jungle. I took that to heart.

One day, I was sitting on the porch with Maw Sunny, swinging my legs and sipping sweet tea, when I said, "The mailman's gonna bring a red envelope today."

She snorted. "Red envelope? Child, we don't even get colored mail."

And she was half right—we didn't.

But ten minutes later, the mailman dropped off a bright red Valentine's card with a gold stamp, addressed to Mama.

"Maw Sunny stared at me, then at the envelope, like she was trying to decide whether I was gifted, cursed, or just plain strange.", then handed me a Popsicle like she wasn't sure if I'd earned a treat or an exorcism.

I didn't think much of it then, but looking back, I wonder if whatever haunted Daddy... brushed off on me too.

I never blamed Daddy, even knowing what I know now.

Because deep in that damaged mind was a man who loved me.

And even when everything else slipped away, that part stayed.

3

High Heels and Haymakers

Monday morning cracked open like an overripe fig.

The house was quiet, but the air was loud—thick with humidity, Aqua Net, and White Diamonds. Not a trace of coffee though. Maw Sunny usually had a pot brewing before sunup, but she was still snoring away on the couch.

Mama was rushing through the hallway, heels clicking like warning shots. She paused at my bedroom door, purse slung at her side, lipstick barely dry, and hung a little hand-smocked dress on the knob—probably one she'd sewn herself, stiff in the sleeves and scratchy around the neck.

"I can't get Maw Sunny up," she called over her shoulder.

"I'm leaving you in charge, Ramey. Make your mama proud now—get yourself ready for school. I have an important job interview at the bank!" She always said that—make your mama proud. Problem was, I never seemed to pull it off. I sat up, my head throbbin' from the faint bruise forming on it—a souvenir

from being dropped like laundry the day before. I rubbed the sore spot, flinching a little, but it didn't ache half as bad as hearing Mama yelling. Always yelling.

Maw Sunny lay sprawled on the couch, bottle still tucked in the crook of her arm like a baby doll. Her snore dragged like a lawnmower through molasses. Mama was stormin' through the place, slammin' cabinets and raisin' hell at nobody in particular.

But I wasn't in the mood for dresses that day. They made it harder to chase down kids at recess—picking on my new buddy. And I wasn't having it. I'd just rip it up anyway or come home caked in mud and shame for messin' up the seam.

I had other plans.

I crept into Mama's room—the one she thought was locked—and picked out my own outfit: a faded gray sweatshirt with a cracked Michael Jackson5 decal, pink short shorts, and those red high heels she kept near the dumbbells.

I didn't know if I wanted to be Tina Turner[9] or Rocky Balboa[10]. Either way, I knew I'd come out swingin'.

In Mama's room, I paused at the posters of Ric Flair on the wall, stood in front the mirror and mouthed his trademark "Whooo" but under my breath so I wouldn't wake Maw Sunny. The weights in the corner were stacked neatly— a reminder that Mama once dreamed of being a bodybuilder before I was born.

I admired her—beautiful, soft-spoken when she wanted, able to use big words and sound so smart. I felt guilty sometimes, thinking maybe my birth had made her give all that up.

I flipped on the old radio hoping to hear something good— and there it was.

♪♫Face to face, out in the heat... hangin' tough, stayin' hungry♪♫... "Aw shit," I whispered. Eye of the Tiger[11]. If I loved a song, I learned every damn word. And this one? This one made

me feel ten feet tall and bayou proof! They were out there staking the odds—but I was ready to take for the kill with the skill to survive.

"Recess was coming, and I was coming for it—with my lil' green tiger eyes. Eyes kind and trusting enough that even adults would share their darkest secrets with me, but fierce enough that I was kickin' ass and takin' names—even back then when I was just a tiny little thing."

I strapped up my tennis shoes, threw Mama's red heels in my book sack—well, just in case.

Because you see, that weekend, I saw my mama do something I'll never forget. We'd pulled up in the rickety black and white striped S-10—didn't even park before she spotted Janice across the street.

Janice—the woman with curlers in her hair and venom in her mouth. The one who'd been runnin' her lips about Maw Sunny to Flip-Flop Face down the way.

Mama slammed it in park right there in the middle of the road, swung the door open, and stepped out like she was walking into a ring. I didn't understand what was about to happen, but something in the way she moved made my chest tighten.

It was terrifying, but fuckin' epic. Like watching a tornado pick its target.

She crossed the street in three strides and, with one clean swing— POW—broke Janice's nose right there in front of God, the neighbors, and the five-year-old sitting in the passenger side.

Blood poured like judgment.

I wanted to vomit right there, choking back the bowl of Corn Flakes I'd just eaten. "Mama, you're bleeding!" She slid back into the truck, calm as a cobra, locked eyes with me, and said: "That's not Mama's blood, baby." I never looked at her the same again. That moment cracked something in

me—like bone splitting open to make room for a weapon. From that day on, I wasn't afraid to swing first.

Now it was Monday. Now I was ready. I just didn't know what for. I just was.

At school, my outfit became instant target practice. Kids laughed, threw paper, poked my barrettes. But none of that mattered. What mattered was

Ace—Ace Bolo, but me and Daddy called him Moose.

A chubby red-haired kid, teased constantly because he had a funny accent. I liked him 'cause he was different—maybe even loved him a little. He smelled like baby powder and peanut butter. I understood him. He understood me. And today, we were gonna face it together.

At recess, Moose was surrounded. The pack of popular kids had him backed up against the rusted monkey bars. They called him "Jam Jello" and "Bozo Bolo." One girl shoved him. Another snatched the book from his hands and tossed it into the mud.

I didn't think. I moved.

Laughter stopped when my high heels clacked onto the concrete. The sound echoed like a ritual bell. They turned. They laughed. "Clown girl! Clown girl!" they chanted. But I didn't flinch. I walked up, eyes fixed on the tallest girl—the alpha. "You want a show?" I whispered. And then I pounced. Barrettes flew. Hair was yanked. One girl screamed. I kicked, scratched, bit.

The scream that tore from my throat wasn't fear—it was ancestral.

Something deep, feral, and older than the school itself.

I was the blood of Sunny Mae.

The daughter of Brinna.

The great-grandchild of Le Guêpe. [12]

"That's not Mama's blood," I thought, wild-eyed.

"But this might be mine."

It took Ace yelling and a teacher sprinting to break it up.

When it was over, my lip was busted and my hair looked like a bird's nest in Hurricane Andrew. My shoes were gone. But Ace was standing. And so was I. We walked to the office together, Ace with his arm around me. I was quiet. Inside, as the teacher cleaned my wound and asked for my mama's number, I answered through a cracked voice:

"Call my daddy."

I received three stitches along the bottom of my lip.

On the drive home, I started fussing about missing the Freedom Assembly at school—paper flags, stapled stars, Mrs. LeBlanc's cassette hissing through "God Bless the U.S.A." They said we were celebrating President Reagan's second term, and I was proud as a firecracker ready to pop.

Daddy kept one hand on the wheel & scratching his neck uneasy with the other,

"Sweet Ramey-baby, he's an actor. It's a show.

"You mean he's not really the president, Daddy?"

"He's the president, sure. But that's the trick—they want you to believe it's yours. Freedom they sell you ain't free. The devil showed 'freedom' in the garden—looked like choice, paid like chains. Ask 'em if they wouldn't hand it back."

He glanced over, softer.

"Come on, I'll get you some ice cream."

When we got home, Maw Sunny was still fast asleep on the couch, front door wide open.

The fact that I had been forced to get myself ready for school at only five years old angered Daddy. It was hard for him to watch his daughter be mistreated. But there wasn't much he could do. If the law got involved, I might end up in foster care, complicating things even more.

"If only I were well enough," I'd hear him say sometimes, "I'd take her."

Once, when I was three, Daddy had found bruises all over my backside, running down to my knees. He took pictures and showed them to his cousin Buck, who was a detective on the bayou.

Buck told him that if he reported it, I'd likely be taken away—and Daddy, due to the severity of his illness, had little chance of winning a fight with the state.

He knew my life was already hard. He wasn't about to throw me into deeper bayou water.

That was all he had left—prayers and regrets. He prayed I'd be okay. Prayed I'd be strong enough for both of us. And deep down, he still hoped his mind would quiet long enough to stay in the fight with me.

That night, after rocking me to sleep and tucking me in, he realized it was getting dark and Mama would be home soon. He smoothed my hair gently and whispered,

"That school best keep a better eye on you… or I'll have to myself."

"I know he left heartbroken, and truth be told, so did I. The hardest part was that whenever Daddy had to leave, it was never our choice. It was always when Mama said, and I know that broke something in both of us."

4

Goose Eggs and Good Intentions

They say the road to hell is paved with good intentions. And if that's true, Mama could've built a six-lane interstate and still had enough leftover asphalt to patch every pothole in St. Fauche Parish.

It wasn't all bad with her. I believe she really did mean well—everything else she touched seemed to turn to gold. But with me, she just had a way of taking the scenic route through the clash. We were oil and water, and no matter how hard she tried, she couldn't make me into what she wanted me to be or give me the life she pictured for me.

The first movie she ever brought me to see was E.T. Mama had a new boyfriend then. I liked him—he was nice, didn't holler or slam doors, just soft-spoken, like maybe he'd been raised in a house where the curtains matched the couch and the couch didn't come from somebody's curb on trash day.

I thought E.T. was the cutest little thing I'd ever seen in my whole four years of life. But when I told Daddy about it, he gave me that slow head shake like I'd just told him I wanted to marry the devil.

"Demons ain't cute, Ramey," he said. "Not till the smell of sulfur fills the air and that slimy finger finds its way where the sun don't shine."

I didn't know what sulfur was, but I figured it must be bad if Daddy was talking about it in his demon voice. And I wasn't sure where the sun didn't shine exactly, but I decided if E.T. ever tried to touch me with that glowing finger, I'd slap it right off his little wrinkly hand.

Mama and her new boyfriend had taken me to see it, trying to do something "family" with me—her way of Mama-ing me into a memory. But the second I came back from Daddy's with his take on it, she got tight-lipped.

"That's why your daddy's sick, Ramey," she said. "He thinks everything is demonic. I can't even try to have fun with you... you and your father take anything I do and make it bad."

One time, at a Mardi Gras Parade down the bayou.
I was riding high on Mama's
shoulders, screaming for beads like a damn fool,
purple and gold feathers slapping me in the face every time she spun around.
Next thing I know—whoosh—I wasn't on her shoulders anymore.
Mama had tripped—drunk as three skunks in a wet paper bag,...
and hit that pavement like a sack of crawfish.
Somebody—don't even know who—caught me midair
before I met the concrete with her.
But Mama? Lord, she took it all.
Big ol' goose egg right in the middle of her forehead,
perfect circle like somebody branded her
with a halo that'd gone sideways.
She laughed it off at first, said,
"I'm fine, baby, I'm fine,"
but the next morning I already knew she was hungover and humiliated.
I still remember her trying to hide that knot with her bangs, my poor Mama
at her new job at the bank.
Folks driving through for cash withdrawals
got a side of shame with their twenties,

and I can picture Mama justa smiling like she wasn't dying inside.

Even then, I remember thinking:

How can someone look so strong and so broken at the same time? Like a china doll holding a switch blade.

Then there was the 1984 World's Fair in New Orleans.

I was only four, but I remember it like a fever dream.

Neon lights everywhere,

the smell of hot dough and powdered sugar,

music rolling off the Mississippi like it belonged to heaven itself.

We rode the carousel till I thought I'd fly off just like E.T.'s bicycle,

ate cotton candy that glued my lil fat cheeks together,

and stared up at that shiny space shuttle like the future had come to N.O.L.A just for us.

And then—of course—I got lost.

One minute Mama's buying us hotdogs,

the next I'm standing there alone, sticky-handed, staring at giants in sunglasses.

Some man asked me where my Mama was at, I said,

"She was drinking a beer and looking at a map, but she fell down at Mardi Gras one time,

so maybe she's on the ground somewhere." shrugging my lil shoulders.

He blinked, scooped me up like a sack of potatoes, and carried me to some security people.

They found Mama near the fountain, crying and fanning herself like she'd lost me for half her life

instead of half an hour.

She hugged me so tight my ribs clicked. "Lord, *Dingbat* you going to be the death of me," she whispered into my hair, and I believed her.

Her boyfriend's family were church-going folks,
Mama went with them on Sundays.
Sat in those pews, lips tight, eyes shiny
like she was holding back every bad word she ever learned.
And just like that—she stopped drinking. Said she was "turning over a new leaf."
For a minute, it almost felt like we might be one of those normal families—
the kind that watch Disney movies
without Daddy calling 'em demonic
and Mama falling face first in the street.
But deep down, I already knew better.
Even as a kid, I could feel how thin that new leaf was—
like one hard rain could wash it clean off the branch.
And sure enough, life has a way of testing every promise you make to yourself.
Daddy had his own ghosts,
his own brick house full of secrets,
and Mama's "new leaf" couldn't hold back
what was already waiting for me on the other side of life.

It didn't make sense to me. How could it? Daddy's demons and Mama's angels spent my whole childhood locked in a tug-of-war for my intellect.

Daddy was a part-time prophet, full-time trouble. Mama ... full-time saint, part-time warden. I guess I was meant to grow up half pure, half feral... and fully fuckin' confused. My little-kid brain was stuck in a joint-custody agreement between Heaven and Hell. No wonder my moral compass spun like a ceiling fan on high.

Daddy warned me about the TV hiding dicks in cartoons,... while he packed his bong. He taught me how to shoot guns and scare the absolute dog-shit out of my little cousin, Buzz. She prayed over the dinner table like God was grading her, then side-eyed my bangs for being two degrees off-center.

Daddy had time for me like it was his only job. Mama worked like she was allergic to sitting still. And me? I was the mess in the middle—trying to read two maps that led to two different heavens, and both of 'em chargin' admission.

In between all that, they programmed me in ways I didn't even notice at the time. Daddy told me to be myself—Flintstone feet and all. He said I had feet like Fred Flintstone, so at five years old I started painting my toenails bright red, figuring if my fat little stone-car-driving feet were gonna stick out, they might as well look like they belonged to a girl.

Mama taught me how to speak with sense, saying "ain't" and "bruh" screams low-class. So I'd scan the room and use my words accordingly.

Daddy taught me that when you meet someone, you squeeze their hand just a touch tighter than they squeeze yours—just enough so they know you ain't no pushover.

One parent told me demons were real and hiding under the bed. The other told me to pick up my room or I'd be the demon.

And still, in the middle of all that confusion, I prayed. As far back as I can remember, I'd been talking to God before we were formally introduced. I talked to God a lot—not because I thought I was special, but because I was always by myself, and well, shit, I like to talk. But mostly because I was in constant need of forgiveness. Everything I liked seemed to be on Hell's playlist.

Like the time I wanted a store-bought dress from Kmart instead of one of Mama's hand-sewn ones for my eight-year-old Catholic communion.

Mama said, "Not no, but hell no, damn heathen!" Said I'd wear one of her

Sew Good specials.

Kmart was twenty minutes away, past the McDonald's and the crack dealers. I knew it was gonna be one of those weekends when Daddy showed up with a Happy Meal and a satin rose clipped to the box—that meant he'd be spending most of the weekend locked in the bathroom. But hallelujah! He said yes. Well, really he said, "Slick, it's your lucky day, it's the 3rd, I can swing it." Shit, I was happier than Richard Simmons sweatin' on old people.

When we got there, I found the dress, he found the problem—pure white lace, tiny veil... crotchless fishnet stockings folded neat on the shelf beneath the busted mannequin with one leg and her privates hangin' out.

Daddy came around the corner just as I held it up, proud as could be. He froze mid-step, eyes wide like he'd seen the rapture happen without us.

"Ramey," he hollered, "put that back. That's not a communion dress, that's for hookers."

I frowned. "But it's white."

"Yeah," he said, "so's cocaine. Now put it back!"

"Well, are your friends Debbie Debutan and Veronica Fisher hookers?"

"No... they're strippers, that's different, Slick. It's their job. They dress up and dance for money."

"Oh, like Madonna!" I said, loud with excitement. I dug my toe, foot up like I had on Mama's red high heels, and tootin' back and forth, pressing it up against my chest, and belted out like a strangled cat:

"Like a verrrrsion—"

He cupped my mouth so tight, lookin' around, then their eyes met—an old lady pushing a buggy full of toilet paper and W.T.F. gave Daddy a look that could've turned water into dog piss.

He tried to defend himself. "It's for church," he said.

She sucked her teeth. "So is confession."

Daddy sighed, "Come on, Slick," steering me toward the children's section. "Ain't no salvation in crotchless fishnets."

For a little while, I had a grandpa. I called him Paw Sleepy, 'cause he napped a lot when he wasn't away at work on the oil rig. He spoiled me rotten. I'd learn later he wasn't even my blood grandpa, but I could've never known it if I hadn't been told—he acted like a real grandpa, unlike Daddy's daddy.

Maw Sunny had married him sometime after Mama's real daddy passed away. Paw Sleepy had been hit head-on by a drunk driver—DOA on La Queue du Diable, "The Devil's Tail," a dark, winding road stitched with trees and ghost stories between St. Faux and Ashroot Parish, where folks still say the land decides who makes it from one side to the next.

I remember Maw Sunny laying his briefcase out on the dining room table like a tombstone. Images from the crash laid strewn across it—shattered glass, drying blood in clumps on the front seat. "Ewe, yuk," I thought.

Then I heard a soft whimper. I followed it through the kitchen to the back of the house. There was a door in the kitchen that led to the utility room where Maw Sunny did laundry. Her back was turned. I watched from the threshold as she hung his ball caps on the clothesline, sunlight pouring through the window warming my face. She didn't sob—just tears, steady as rain, as she turned and looked my way. I'd never seen her cry before… not like Mama, who cried herself to sleep most nights.

That was my first sting of loss by death. My grandpa was never coming back. I remember telling God over and over, "I'm scared of dying, Father. I don't want to die." I'd shut my eyes and let the light find me. It wasn't loud—it crept in like mist, like something holy but quiet. I could feel sleep pulling me under, slow as syrup, and then I'd wake up with the sun on my face, like God had sent an angel to keep watch ore' me through the night.

I was nine when I prayed for snow. Mama said Louisiana didn't do that—not since she was a little girl.

But I begged God anyway, whispered it like a secret deal in the dark. And I'll be damned if—

Cane fields dressed in lace, ice clinging to every fence post like heaven had dipped us in sugar.

Folks said it was coincidence. Not me. Still to this day, nobody can tell me it wasn't my prayer. I know it was.

And even if it wasn't, my belief that it was became one of those mustard seeds Jesus talked about—small enough to fit in a child's palm, strong enough to split mountains if you held it tight.

That snow was proof in my pocket, and it kept me believing long after other folks would've folded their hands and walked away from God empty.

5

As Long As I'm Alive

After being raised by Maw Sunny for the first eight years of my life, the thought of moving to a new home with my mama and her new husband scared me a little. No more breakfast in bed, no more wringing chicken necks all day with my ol' maw maw. But I was hopeful.

Our new two-bedroom shotgun house was in a rough neighborhood nicknamed Atomic Lane for all the troublemakers who lived there. Before the move, Maw Sunny had tried to give me hope about starting over at a new school, making new friends. Even though it was hard for her to let me go, she wanted me to be with mama, hoping it would strengthen our bond.

Her drinking had slowed down a bit, but when it hit, it still landed hard—and never spared my lil' self esteem.

That night I sat on the new couch watching Rainbow Brite with a bowl of cereal. I heard her crying in the other room. At first, I ignored it, but eventually I got up, wanting to comfort her. I moved too quickly and spilled the rest of my cereal on the new furniture. I was clumsy in that way. The bowl hit the floor with a loud clatter.

She burst out of the bedroom and found me scooping soggy cereal with my hands.

"You are not going to come over here and start ruining my new things! You ruin everything—" she

screamed, and kicked the dog shit outta me.

"I'm sorry, Mama! Really, I'm sorry!" My stomach turned at the rage in her eyes.

I learned to block out the pain early. Close my eyes and follow the light.

"Oh, you think you're tough now, huh?"

One second I was there, gone the next. Something split my nerves wide open,...

I was back, now standing outside

myself, staring down at the body I'd just left, poor pathetic thing staring blankly right back at me!

Scared the shit out of me. Whatever flashed in my eyes—fear, defiance, *DEATH* must've scared the shit out of her too. She froze, dropped the board I had assumed was her long man foot, and ran out the house sobbing.

Inside my body on the floor my brain in the fog.

I limped to the phone and dialed.

"Daddy?"

Before I could say more, she stormed back in, snatched the receiver from my hand. Daddy's voice bled through the line. Her face twisted.

"Oh, you think you're cute calling your crazy-ass daddy?" she slurred.

I stayed quiet. Didn't want hear her mouth.

She slammed the phone down, grabbed her keys, and jerked me toward the door.

"Come on," she snapped. "You wanna go to your crazy-ass daddy? I'll take you there myself."

The whole ride was silent but for her ragged breathing. Me floating alongside myself half the ride. I held my

breath every time her knuckles went white on the steering wheel, half sure she'd throw me out the window or crash us both.

When we pulled into Daddy's driveway, she didn't wait. She dragged me out.

Daddy was standing on the porch. His eyes narrowed. I broke free, ran to him just as she lunged. He said later he didn't

remember grabbing the axe by the door—only raising it high, his voice shaking with fury.

"Three seconds to get off my property."

She froze, mascara running down her cheeks, voice breaking between rage and despair:

"Ughhh—I can't take this! You think you're clean, Levi Roland? You're part of it too!"

She spat curses at him, at me.

But she turned and left.

Daddy dropped the ax as I watched Mama leave La Guêpe St.

When you turned down the street, you were on La Guêpe territory.

Every home down the street there family

owned. It was the kind of place people called ours, with both pride and a hint of warning.

Anita Roland's land—Daddy's grandma. Daddy named her La Guêpe, the french word for wasp. We just called her *"The Gep"*.

Daddy had a name for er'body. It fit her perfectly. She was short, wiry, sharp-tongued, and so strong she could throw

cousin Buzz over one shoulder, slap Jasmine upside her head with a fly swatter, and threaten to sew up my

bottom for pissin' on everything—without skipping a beat.

When Daddy's daddy, my blood grandpa, ran off with another woman, Anita disowned her own son and helped raise

Daddy and his siblings. She never forgave betrayal, and she ruled that street with the same sting that gave her her nickname.

Now Grandpa Lucian himself had been a complicated man. Local barber, pawn shop owner, hotel manager, grocer, local bus driver. He wore more hats than the racks at the thrift store. And in darker corners of town, people whispered about the dope sold out of his pawn shop and the women he pimped out of it.

Daddy carried those whispers with him. He hated the man for what he did to their family. But like everything else in this parish, hate and love tangle together like roots in the mud.

Now, the old brick house was Daddy's childhood home. Three bedrooms. Tall ceilings that held heat in the summer like a kiln. In the back hall was his old bedroom—that last door on the left, a museum of pain he rarely entered.

On the windowsill were hundreds of carved notches. One for every time grandpa's belt buckle cut into him after he'd told his mother the truth about Miss Mabel. He tattled, yes—and he'd pay for it in blood and bruises, keeping his own record right there in the wood.

He ran a hand along the windowsill, showing me the notches carved deep in the wood.

"See these?" Daddy said, running his finger over them. "That's every day I made it through in here." He glanced at me, his eyes glassy but steady. "I brought you in here so you'd know I really understand what you're going through. I don't want you getting sick from what I went through. You're too good for that."

"This is where he'd beat me. I used to count every time that belt came down. I made these just to piss him off. He worshipped this big red brick house like it proved something. Said he wanted us to have better than he ever did—guess he saved all that for his new wife and kids."

He exhaled slowly, staring past me like he saw something else. Then, almost to himself, he muttered:

"Don't you ever trust the bayou."

I tilted my head. "Why?"

He pulled me close, voice low, steady.

"Bayou'll take what it wants and never give it back. You fall in, it don't matter if you scream—water'll close over you like you were never here."

To me, the bayou was just frogs, crawfish traps, and gator eyes glowing at night. But Daddy wasn't warning me about swimming. He was warning me about something bigger.

"They like it 'cause it don't leave no proof," he whispered, almost like he forgot I was there. "Bayou swallows sins whole."

"Well, who are they?" I asked.

"That's the thing, Slick—who knows. Might be the president, might be the devil, might be aliens."

"What if it's all of them?" I asked.

No answer.

After a long silence, he shook himself and sighed.

"Come on. Let's get out of this room."

He carried me to the living room, settling me into the old rocker and pulling a quilt around me.

"You want to hear some music?"

I nodded.

He rummaged through his records and found Hank Williams Sr.

"If anything happens to me, remember to play this at my funeral," he said.

"I know, Daddy."

He smiled, voice catching. "That's my girl."

Ramblin' Man crackled through the old player as he rocked me slowly, feeling my breathing ease.

"That's how they count you out, baby girl. Not in hours. Not in days. Just in waiting. Whole life slips past

while you're still sittin' in the same chair, thinkin' you're safe."

He stroked my hair, staring at the dead clock.

"If that thing ever starts ticking again, you run. Don't wait. Don't ask. Just run."

I nodded. It was just another one of Daddy's strange sayings, like talking to Eric or cussing at shadows.

After a while, I stirred against his chest.

"Daddy… I wanna tell Eric goodnight."

He looked over at the shelf where the old ceramic skull sat, its blue doll eyes open and staring.

"Good idea," Daddy said softly.

He handed it to me. I kissed its cold forehead and laid it on its side so the eyes clicked shut.

"Goodnight, Eric," I whispered.

for a moment, the room went still. Daddy's eyes flicked to the skull like it acknowledged me—and then,

clear as a voice carried on a breath:

Goodnight, Ramey.

Daddy swallowed hard and smiled down at me.

"Eric says goodnight too, baby girl," he whispered, pulling me closer.

I smiled, hugging him tight.

Eric might've been a little skull head, but he was mine too—my big brother of sorts, because Daddy never

had a girlfriend, never gave me brothers or sisters. Eric was special to him, and so he was special to me.

And that night, Daddy kept rocking, one arm around me, one hand resting on Eric like we were all family.

Life, I'd learn later, is kinda like those 3-D posters they sold at the mall—

you don't see a damn thing staring

at it. But if you soften your eyes, look through instead of at, a whole hidden picture rises clear as day.

Sometimes I wonder if that's what I was doing that night—looking too close at Daddy's love and not

through it to see the curse curled underneath.

And I can't help but wonder: by kissing that creepy-ass skull

goodnight, did I call something over? Or were we damned regardless?

"Do not bring a detestable thing into your house or you, like it, will be set apart for destruction. Regard it as vile

and utterly detest it, for it is set apart for destruction." — Deuteronomy 7:26

6

E.R.I.C., The Watcher

How Eric came to be :

Daddy used to say he was a soldier, but even back then something didn't add up. Records later showed he'd only served one month in the actual military, barely long enough to break in a pair of boots. By then, the windowsill already carried the proof of what kind of discipline he'd grown up under.

And if that torment wasn't bad enough, after getting expelled for punching a nun at boarding school, his daddy had shipped him to boot camp.

Only this wasn't the kind with drills and medals. Part of it, he swore, was administered at none other than Haunt-Bourne Medical/ The Nut House—a place more hospital ward than barracks, where discipline came in the form of wires, pills, and tests ain't nobody volunteered for.

That's where he said he first crossed paths with what he called a majestic soldier. Not the kind of man you salute, but the kind who made your blood run cold. A G-Man type. One of those government phantoms who never answered questions—only asked them.

Daddy claimed the man handed him Eric like it was both a gift and a dare, leaning in to whisper:

"You'll know when it starts talking."

"And somewhere in between the acid eye drops and them zappin' me like a mosquito trap, I guess he was conjured.

I named him Eric," Daddy said, "'cause he likes Marvin."

He told me those eyes weren't store-bought. Said they came off a baby doll left in his dorm.

"Couldn't stand it starin' at me like that," he said. "So I carved 'em out and gave 'em a new home."

He tapped Eric's forehead.

"Now he sees for both of us."

He named the skull Eric after the talking skull from Dr. Marrowbine Marvin that strange late-night show on WW-ELFs-TV out of New Orleans. Most folks thought Marvin was just campy horror—a mad scientist and his wise-cracking skull sidekick telling bad jokes between movies. But Daddy treated it like a sacred origin story, as though Eric wasn't just from television, but from the same hidden current that had pulled him through Haunt-bourne.

"Every good scientist needs a skull that tells the truth, Slick," he'd say, tapping Eric's forehead like it might blink back at him.

Eric wasn't the only thing they gave him. There was a book too—stamped Roland across the spine, dated December 1980 with an official certification and Daddy's name inside. He said it was a souvenir, a parting gift, something he was supposed to pass on to a son he swore he'd never have.

He used to joke about it, calling it the government's little mercy.

"They broke my baby-maker right along with my brain, Slick," he'd laugh.

The pills, the wires, the shocks—they'd rewired more than his mind. Whatever they pumped through him left him sterile, and hollow in places men aren't supposed to be.

"Guess I wasn't built for that kinda love," he said once, lighting another Kool. "They took that, too. Only thing I ever felt close to after that besides you, was a carton of these, or maybe a party ball if the money was right."

Sometimes I wondered if that's why he clung so hard to Eric—that skull didn't just talk; it listened. It was safe. Didn't ask for touch, didn't need forgiveness. Maybe he built it so he wouldn't have to be alone with what they'd taken.

"All those years in that program, and all I got was an honorable discharge, a creepy skull, and a book for a son I'll probably never meet."

He smirked.

"Could've at least given me a damn T-shirt. Hell, Uncle Sam could've sprung for a good pocket tee. One I could've kept my Kools in."

The Night Eric Mistook the Beignets for the Enemy

I remember one evening, Daddy decided to play chef. He'd hauled out Mama's old cast-iron skillet, a sack of powdered sugar he had retrieved from a box on the front porch, and a bag of flour he nicked from the grocery store when nobody was looking.

Daddy standing there at the stove, grease popping in Mama's old skillet, powdered sugar hanging in the air like Scarface sneezed all over the damn place. Me and Buzz leaned over the counter, watching Daddy—see what this fool about to do.

Daddy grabbed the sack, dumped the heap into the bowl, and doing the worst Cuban accent I ever heard, yelled:

"Say hello to my little beignet!"

Buzz nearly toppled.

"Uncle Levi, you're so crazy!"

"I know that's right, Buzzy Boy! So crazy they pay me for it!" Daddy replied.

"Buzz, hush your face," I whispered. I was laughing so hard my belly hurt.

That's when Eric must have said something, because all of a sudden Daddy spun around cock-eyed to the right and back. Spatula froze mid-air. His face went pale, eyes darting to the skull's baby-blue doll eyes like they'd just barked an order at him he wasn't happy about.

Before I knew what was happening, he grabbed that spatula, handled it as if it was a rifle, and bolted for the back door—powdered sugar flying everywhere.

I scrambled behind him, half laughing, half terrified, wondering what the hell he's about to get us into today. Daddy swung that screen door open, leveled the spatula, and shouted:

"Show yourselves, you powdered fiends!"

The only thing on the porch was Ole Miss Delacroix's pet cat, Toulouse, sitting smugly on the step with a sugar-coated whisker. She yawned, flicked her tail, and strode off as if she'd just watched a madman armed with a frying pan declare war on pastries.

Inside, Daddy stomped back to the stove, cheeks red enough to fry an egg on. He tapped Eric's forehead, muttering:

"Next time, warn me before the french Resistance comes gunning for my sugar stash."

Then he sighed, plated me with fresh beignets—sugar and all. He winked and said:

"See? Nothing to fear but a warm beignet and a fat cat with sticky paws."

Even now, whenever I smell fried dough, I half expect Eric to manifest himself through the sweet aroma.

The Water Talk

Eric rattled loud enough to make Daddy stop cold. He narrowed his eyes like the skull had just whispered an insult again.

"That bastard. He hid the remote," he muttered. "He's taunting me. Thinks I can't find it."

He snapped his head toward me.

"Slick, grab that shoe polish and call Buzz in here."

I blinked.

"For what?"

"War paint, Slick. You think we go into battle bare-faced like some damn tourists?"

Next thing I know, Daddy is smearing black shoe polish all across my cheeks like I'm Rambo's half-pint sidekick. Buzz comes skidding in, and Daddy does the same to him—straight line across his forehead, two streaks down the cheeks. Buzz salutes like G.I. Joe with a Kool-Aid mustache.

"All right," Daddy said, crouching low, whispering like we were behind enemy lines. "Eric hid the remote. Our mission: break him. first, we secure the prisoner."

The prisoner was Eric, who Daddy plunked into the baby carriage like he was about to stand trial. Then Daddy dragged us into The Gep's garage, rummaging like raccoons on meth, and came out with a cardboard box, a busted box cutter, and duct tape.

"This," he announced, "is our paddy wagon."

Buzz scrambled inside the box, grinning like an idiot. I taped it crooked while Daddy supervised, nodding like Patton. When it was done, he dropped it over Eric in the carriage, patted it twice, and said:

"Now we interrogate."

We rolled the rig into the yard, neighbors watching us from across the street like we were the opening act of a nervous breakdown. Daddy hooked up the garden hose, aimed it right at Eric's nose hole, and growled:

"Drip it slow, Slick. Don't drown him too fast. We need intel."

Buzz twisted the nozzle with both hands, letting water drip in one slow plop at a time. Daddy pressed his ear against the skull like it was a conch shell.

"He's cracking..." Daddy whispered. "Cushion. Couch. Under."

He shot up, eyes wild.

"Couch cushions! MOVE OUT!"

Me and Buzz tore inside like lunatics, shoe polish streaking down our faces, eyes burning like hell, flipping cushions like we were raiding a crack den. And there it was—the remote, grinning up at us from under the armrest.

We ran back inside, holding it high like Olympic gold. Daddy snatched it, held it aloft, and declared:

"Mission accomplished. Prisoner broken."

Then he shook Eric like a wet dog, wrapped him in a towel like a disgraced P.O.W., and plopped him on the sofa between me and Buzz. He tossed Buzz a victory bowl of popcorn, clicked the remote, and barked:

"Now we watch *faces of Death*—for the troops."

I sat down, greasy black streaks still across my cheeks, munching popcorn while wondering how the hell a skull could hide a remote in the first place—and if we were supposed to salute before or after they smashed the monkey head and ate the brains.

Most people would've tossed the thing in the trash. But Daddy kept Eric on the windowsill and the book locked away in a drawer. He swore Eric spoke when trouble was coming—loud as a thunderclap rollin' down the bayou.

Nobody else ever heard it, but Daddy always did. And he repeated every word out loud like he'd just been handed marching orders.

Sometimes it was one sharp word, sometimes a whole rant. And Daddy worked it into one of those cock-eyed campaigns that always seemed to end up at some ridiculous, half-baked adventure.

And more O.F.T.E.N.[13] , than not, turned out truer than we ever wanted to believe.

Hard to tell if Daddy was just bored, high, or bat-shit crazy.

But Eric's whisper lingered *: watch the road by the old oak; a shot's only a punctuation in a sentence already written.*

"Daddy...say what?"

We still listened.

7

The Cost to Kill a Badge

In 1989, I walked through two houses that taught me more than any school, church, or courtroom ever could.

One smelled like gumbo, orange zest, and secrets cooked slow. The other smelled like scorched wood and fresh coffee. One held ghosts in silk suits. The other held a sheriff who'd just outran death. And in both places, I was just a little girl—watching, remembering, being quiet.

We were at Noose Neck Nolan's place—Daddy's daddy's side. We just called him Uncle Noose. That side of the family had land, legacy, and long shadows. The kind of house where deals didn't happen on paper, and silence was its own form of inheritance.

That's when Daddy leaned down to me and said: "Hey, Slick… you know who that is?" "No, Daddy, who is it?" "That's The Godfather of New Orleans."

But Daddy died before I got old enough to hear the who, what, why, and how. Still and all—that whisper—it never left me. Some years later, in a history class, they dropped the name. Mob connections. Backroom alliances dressed up as politics. And when the teacher showed his picture? I recognized him immediately. Same fat jaw. Same devious smile. I could even smell his cologne. And I remember thinking he had a lot of hangnails for a man in a suit.

That same week, Daddy pressed a starched shirt against his chest like it was armor. "We're goin' upriver, Slick. Mississippi." His eyes glinted, with obligation. Uncle Noose had "business"—and that business looked like a casino steamboat with chandeliers that swayed like they were seasick, docked where the river itself bent to listen.

The celebration wasn't for the public. No flyers, no parade. Just men in linen suits with rings heavy as anchor chains, their laughter rolling louder than the paddle wheel itself. Women in feathers and sequins drifted through smoke like moving tarot cards. Every deck smelled of bourbon, gumbo, and polished wood—but underneath it, something sharper. Ozone. Static. Like the air right before lightning strikes.

When Daddy walked me past the card tables, men tipped their hats, but none of them looked me in the eye. Not really. Their gazes slid over me like glass, landing instead on the way Daddy held my hand too tight, the way Uncle Noose whispered in his ear with the casual menace of someone who never had to raise his voice.

At some point in the night, a man in a red bow tie stooped down to my height, touched my chin, and said, "She's a quiet one. Strong jaw. Good lungs too, I bet." He laughed, and I missed the punchline. Later I learned he wasn't joking. Daddy pulled me back, muttered "watch yourself," and Noose smoothed it over with a toast.

The show came next. A troupe of kids—maybe ten, maybe more—poured onto the stage in satin and sequins, bows tight, cheeks rouged like apples. They moved together like one long ribbon, feet kissing the boards in time. I thought lucky. Wished Mama would put me in dance or cheer or anything with a matching costume and hair sprayed still, instead of that poverty ponytail she swore "built character."

The band played bright, and the lights made their smiles look expensive. A man with a little black book stood at the edge like he was keeping score for the show. Each kid stepped into a circle of light and struck a pose, and the grown-ups clapped and tossed chips like confetti. I clapped too, palms stinging, trying to catch the rhythm like I belonged to it.

Daddy said the captain gave us a room "fit for river royalty." The hallway was long and yellow. Every step made the floor moan. He opened the door, proud, like he'd built it himself. "See that, Slick? Our own quarters." It was bad ass.

I ran my hand across the quilt. Fancy shit here podna. Somebody hollered from down the hall—his name sharp in the air. "Levi! They need you up top!" Daddy sighed, rubbed the back of his neck. "Lock up behind me, alright? I'll be back before you miss me." He dropped the keys in my hand. Heavy. Warm. Then he was gone.

I dug around eating junk, flipping through the massive idiot box, then I heard it. The sink gurgled once, then twice, then made a sound that didn't belong to pipes. A soft cluck. Then another. I waited for it to stop, but it didn't. The sound crawled through drain pipe. I opened the door to our room, then I seen it—a slit in the wall near the corner. Not quite a door, not quite nothing. Like somebody tried to seal it shut and changed their mind halfway through.

I should've stayed put. But I didn't. I never did.

I pulled it—of course I did, couldn't help it. The panel peeled back slow, exhaling heat and bleach and something sweet enough to rot teeth. A narrow staircase twisted down below deck. That's when I saw a small door, cracked just enough to tempt me. I thought it was a closet—maybe candy, maybe something better. But behind it was a locked room, letters stenciled in red: Hühner[14].

At first, nothing. Then—thud. A pause. Another thud. Then a cheer, muffled and wrong. And over it all, the sound of chickens.

Before I could lean closer, Daddy's voice ripped through the dark. "Ramey, what the hell are you doing?" He hauled me back up through the crawlspace, breath sharp. "Daddy… what are they doing down there?" He didn't answer right away. Just stared at the slit in the wall like he'd found a crack in heaven's floorboards. "I don't know," he said finally, voice low. "And I don't wanna know. That ain't a door for us, Slick. You hear me? You don't open it again."

He pulled the panel shut like sealing a wound, then locked it with a key I hadn't seen him use before. The next few days blurred by—so much food, so much noise. The paddle wheel kept churning, the chickens kept clucking, but nobody brought it up again. Not Daddy. Not me. It was like the whole boat agreed: some doors stay shut.

A week later — different house.

Different bloodline.

We were at Grom's house — Daddy's mama's side.

The side that raised Buck like their own.

Buck, who wore the badge and carried the weight of it, I'm sure.

The coffee was on, the gumbo steaming, when the television cut into the afternoon with a bulletin. Voices low and steady:

"Sheriff Ronin Lukeroy is expected to live after being shot late last night.

His condition is serious, and no timetable has been set for a return to duty.

An acting sheriff will be named while the investigation continues. Two men are in custody; nearly thirty questioned."

The room went still. No one moved but Grom, ladling gumbo into bowls like Sunday didn't care about snipers. She didn't look up when she said it: "I told y'all all that pryin' gonna get somebody killed. Levi, you ain't helpin' nothin'—stirrin' a hornet nest with a soup spoon. God knows what you fillin' that sheriff's head up with."

Buck stared straight ahead, shoulders squared like stone. Daddy sipped his coffee slow, his silence louder than words. I leaned close, my child's voice breaking the hush. "Did the sheriff get hurt bad?" Daddy set his cup down, eyes fixed somewhere far off. "Well," he said dryly, "I suppose… since it almost took him clean out." And that was all.

No details. No explanations. Only the news repeating a number that thudded like a pulse: $10,666. That was the price on Sheriff Ronin Lukeroy's head. Not ten grand. Not eleven. $10,666. A number soaked in symbolism and blood. A mockery of justice. A message only the initiated were supposed to understand.

10 — law and judgment. 666 — corruption and control. Together, hmm—that's the cost to kill a badge, bebe.

8

Big Brothers' Watching

Daddy's Place Was the Spot If there was one thing he did best, it was drawing people in.

Bikers, shrimpers, strippers, old friends, new faces—his door stayed open, and the party never really stopped.

He never did get another girlfriend after Mama, but he didn't need one. Every weekend he'd grin that sideways grin and say, "Got a party ball and an 8-ball. You ready to party?" to whoever was hanging around.

Honestly? Sounded fun to me.

Mama was so serious all the time. At home she could hardly crack a smile. She'd cry herself to sleep some nights. I wished she'd been more like Daddy. He made you forget the world for a while.

She used to tell me, "I used to be fun. You and your daddy sucked the fun right out of me."

I guess she had to do the grown-up stuff Daddy wouldn't. She resented him for that.

They were both Cancers, too—born a week apart. Two crabs in one pot.

And their fights? They were the stuff of legend.

Uncle Vince told me a story about when they were only eighteen. Daddy had this expensive blue pit bull—named Blue, of course. Mama hated that dog because it was sick with worms and shitting giant piles everywhere in the house.

Vince said he watched her sitting on the steps with a bottle of Jack in her hand, waiting for Daddy to pull up. As soon as he did, she took a last swig, grabbed the dog's collar, pulled out her .22, and blasted Blue right there in front of him.

I knew it was true, because Mama always said Daddy didn't care about the mess, or the animals. She told me about his spider monkey that would throw shit at her and how Daddy would just laugh and laugh.

But my Mama had her own mean streak.

I remember being seven and finding her stuffing newborn kittens in a ziplock bag.

"Mama, what are you doing?"

"Mercy kill, Ramey," she said, pushing the air out before zipping it tight. "They been crying all day. Their mama's gone. Now they go to Jesus faster."

She tossed them in the trash like it was nothing. That always stuck with me.

Daddy was no saint either. He once told me he and Mama dropped acid together. She had a big aquarium she loved, all lit up. Daddy thought it'd be funny to shut off all the house lights and switch the fish tank on, yelling, "Look, Brinna! I'm walking on water!" before crashing straight through it.

Needless to say, that backyard turned into a Mercy Kill Cemetery.

But that was them. Explosive. Messy. Funny as hell and mean as hell.

Daddy called the TV the "idiot box." Hardly turned it on unless it was for The Three Stooges or Marvin.

God, I loved those old shows. I'd make him pretend he was Chobley[15] and I'd be Marvin, of course. Eric… well, he was Eric—he didn't get a choice.

We used to pull the best pranks. One of my favorites was on Buzz, my po lil' cousin. Daddy would flip his eyelids inside out, showing nothing but the white of his eyeballs, his false teeth hanging halfway out of his mouth lookin' like a loon.

I'd go running to Buzz yelling, "Oh no! Buzz, come see! I think Eric killed Daddy!"

We'd have Eric laid out with a plastic knife in his mouth, Daddy playing corpse with those teeth and eyes all crazy. Then *The Genius*—Daddy's bestest childhood podna—would sneak in with a blow horn and this fake turd.

He'd blast the horn and hurl the turd at us while Daddy cracked open the fart spray capsule.

Buzz would be holding the fake turd all confused and horrified right before the smell hit him.

I guess the joke was on us all, cause bae bae, when that smell would hit, we'd all gag so hard we were falling over laughing and holding back puke. Good times, I tell ya. Even Buzz would wind up laughing, whining:

"You got me, Uncle Levi! Ga darn it!"

Daddy and *The Genius*—those two fools were something else. He'd been a schoolteacher but quit because he made more money shrimping in the summers than all year in the classroom. He ended up buying a bigger boat and making millions off the Gulf.

The Genius was one of Daddy's only straight friends besides Buck the detective. Everyone else? Wild as hell.

Bikers. Strippers. Junkies. Suited men with slick hair and weird smiles.

Daddy's friends came from every walk of life. And me? I was usually the only kid, right there with them, soaking it all in.

They didn't do drugs in front of me. They didn't have to. I was always listening. Always watching. And I had a memory like barbed wire—it caught on certain things and never let go.

If I saw your hands or your feet once, it was stamped permanent in my mind forever, whether I wanted it there or not. I knew what people's feet looked like down to their weird toenails. No foot fetish—more like the opposite. feet grossed me out.

Funny thing was, I couldn't figure out algebra to save my life—or my ass with Mama. Numbers slipped through me like water, but details stuck like tattoos.

Years later I'd find out I was dyslexic, which explained plenty, but back then ain't nobody caught it. All I knew was my brain worked like a busted camera—blind to some things, laser-etched on others.

Daddy spent half his disability check on drugs and the other half on fart spray and fake poo from a little souvenir shop in faux-chon, right before the beach.

God, I loved that place. Crack pipes in the glass case right next to gag gifts.

He'd say, "Come on, Slick, let's go get some supplies."

He was so silly—even with The Gep, my great-grandmother.

One time we were at the grocery store. The Gep was pushing the buggy while Buzz and I were on one side and Daddy was on the other.

Daddy caught my eye, gave me that conspirator nod like, "Watch this shit and hold my beer."

He reached over and pinched that long, sagging skin under The Gep's arm, then hollered real loud:

"Aww, Buzz! Don't do that to your old grandma!"

The Gep spun on Buzz so fast. She started wailing on him with that old lady strength, shouting, "Don't squeeze my meat, Buzz! Stop squeezing my meat!"

Me and Daddy were howling laughing, tears streaming down our faces. Poor Buzz was crying real tears too, but for a different reason, while Daddy had to pull The Gep off of him. She threatened to throw Buzz in the bayou.

We about died laughing. Even po Buzz finally cracked a smile after a while.

We had music running nonstop. Rap was taking over the world, and Daddy mostly stayed in his old-country lane, but he tried to be cool for us kids.

He was an old hippie at heart—long hair, scruffy beard, pocket T-shirt stuffed with Kool cigarettes and a lighter, cheap strap-on tennis shoes, and a ball cap.

He looked ridiculous as hell, dry-humping the air like a fool whenever *funky Cold Medina* came on MTV.

Then he'd nod at the idiot box and mumble, "Big Brother's watching," in that half-joking, half-serious voice of his.

I didn't understand it back then.

"That's what it's made for, Slick."

But to me? Back then, it was just funny.

We'd hang out listening to records, and he'd call me over.

"Ramey, come here. Look in that peephole."

I'd climb up on a chair, press my eye to it—and outside he'd start dancing to *Groove Is in the Heart,* moving closer and further away like the video with the fisheye lens. Hat off, hair shaking, being ridiculous. I'd be howling.

Other times, I'd be outside with a friend and hear a ghostly voice calling our names. We'd look everywhere and finally spot him peeking through a window, grinning like a loon.

He loved scaring the shit out of us.

And when it wasn't pranks, it was jokes about Eric. He'd lay that skull down gently and say, "Go to sleep, Eric. He won't shut up unless I cover him up."

He'd even put a sheet over him, deadpan serious, just to make me laugh.

It wasn't all sunshine. He had a dark side. He ran with some sketchy crowds. There were rumors about mob ties, though I could never prove anything.

But I saw enough shady deals, enough men in suits, enough bottom-of-the-barrel motherfuckers that I wouldn't rule it out.

I remember one night clear as day. I was in my room playing Barbies when this strange man in a long trench coat burst in and started toward me.

I froze.

Before he could take another step, Rob—one of Daddy's shrimp-boat friends—stormed in. Rob was solid muscle from hauling nets. He grabbed that guy in a headlock and dragged him out the door like a sack of crawfish.

Women came running in, big blonde hair and bigger tits.

"Baby, you alright?"

Daddy came in behind them, laughing but pissed.

"If he dies, we'll feed him to the gators!"

He shooed everyone out, then crouched by me.

"I'm sorry, Ramey. I don't know what that creep thought he was doing. But you know I'd never let anything happen to you."

When the house finally went quiet, Daddy went still. His eyes glazed over in Eric's direction, Kool smoke swirling around his beard from his nostrils.

"Nothing happens by accident, baby," he said. "Men up high pull strings—make you dance, make you bleed—and clap like it was your idea."

I just chalked it up to crazy talk; wasn't sure what that had to do with the man in the trench coat, but hey, I felt safe with him.

funny, wild, and dangerous if you crossed the wrong line—that was Daddy.

And me? I worshiped the ground he walked on. No matter how loud the party got, he made space for me. He made me laugh. And for a little while—before the world fell apart—that was enough.

I didn't understand everything that was going on back then, but I always felt safe with him.

9

Keeping Secrets Keeps You Safe

The counselor clicked her marker against the dry erase board and wrote in big block letters:

SECRETS KEEP YOU SICK.

I copied it into my notebook like a good little girl, nodding at all the right times. But deep down? I knew the real truth: *Secrets keep you safe.*

I didn't grow up in a family that sat around talking about our feelings. We talked around things. Or over things. Or drank them down. Some of us held it in so long it turned to rot—ate through our guts, cracked our minds, and showed up as ghosts behind our eyes. Others let them out sideways—through fists, belts, silence, or vanishing.

But we didn't talk. Not really. And if we did? Someone might end up dead. Or worse—disowned.

Down here, it's not just blood that runs deep. It's loyalty. It's history. It's the kind of silence you inherit.

You don't ask why Uncle Noose started planting orange trees the same year the New Orleans Godfather got out of prison. You just learn where not to park your bike.

You don't ask why there's still burn marks on the side of Maw Maw's shed. You just know to get quiet when certain names come up.

And when your last name shows up in a newspaper next to the words *attempted assassination*? You learn real quick how to keep your damn mouth shut.

It wasn't just the big things we didn't talk about. It was the little ones too.

Like why Aunt Lurlene kept a shotgun in the umbrella stand.

Or why my cousin Jace flinched every time someone said *Fourth of July.*

Or why Maw Maw's recipe box had a false bottom with two Polaroids and a folded-up letter that smelled like motor oil.

We didn't ask. We just learned to read the room. To clock the mood before we walked in. To know when to laugh loud and when to disappear.

I used to think silence was just something you did to survive. But down here? Silence is a skill. A currency. A weapon. And if you master it early enough, you get to keep your seat at the table.

I seen 'em on Sundays—pressed shirts, polished smiles, and them red leather shiny shoes. But I knew those shoes weren't for the Lord's work. They were for midnight mass, the kind held behind the shed, where no one said *Amen* and the candles smelled like secrets ain't nobody ever repeating.

It wasn't that I didn't want to scream. I just knew better.

One side of my family had cops—real ones. Detectives. Men who were raised by my great-grandma like sons and still came by to kiss her on the cheek and eat cornbread straight out the cast iron.

The other side? People passing envelopes, whispering about shipments and favors. Not one wore the same badge, but everybody knew their position—best believe it.

And then there was me—

A little girl sitting on a foldout lawn chair watching people play dominoes like they were rolling dice on who lived and who got silenced next.

The air smelled like sweat, beer, and stinky cigars. Somebody always had a story, but nobody ever told the whole thing. Just enough to make you wonder. Just enough to make you scared.

One time I asked Uncle Darnell what happened to the man with the limp who used to bring Maw Maw pecan pralines.

He looked at me, real slow, and said:

"He forgot who he owed."

Then he cracked a domino down so hard the table shook, and nobody said another word.

I kept their secrets because they were mine too.

Because I didn't want to be the next body they stopped crying about.

Because I didn't want to get anyone killed.

Because I loved them—even the ones who didn't deserve it.

Because when I talked, I got punished.

When I told the truth, I got left.

When I opened up, people shut down.

When I screamed, people got scared.

When I stayed silent? I got to stay, and I got to play dominoes too.

Now that I'm older, I've learned: there's more than one kind of death.

There's the kind where your body stops working—

and the kind where your spirit gets erased in small pieces every time you bite your tongue when someone tells the story wrong.

Maybe I was born into a name that got printed next to an attempted assassination.

Maybe my Daddy stood in a room with men who never got photographed.

Maybe I smiled at the ones who whispered orders with gravy on their breath.

And maybe I loved them—and hated them—at the same time.

But Daddy? Daddy loved Sheriff Ronin Lukeroy.

When he found out one of the hit men had our last name—Roland—it lit him up. Said:

"That ain't us. Don't you dare lump me in with that bullshit."

He was pissed. Not just because of what happened—

but because someone tried to drag our blood into it.

And that? That was unforgivable.

I didn't know why he was so worked up until one night, hiding behind the hallway heater vent, knees to my chest like when Maw Sunny had company I didn't trust.

One of those men said it, voice low and heavy like a stone dropped in water:

"I know you're upset, son, but you did the honorable thing. You served your country in ways that go beyond the field. But we can't use Ramey like this. She's marked."

Marked. The word rang in my head like a church bell.

"She's got that light," the man added. "Same as you. We can't risk interference, we'll need to..."

Daddy's chair creaked, cutting him off mid-sentence. His voice came sharp as broken glass:

"You leave my girl alone. Whatever deal you had with my daddy back in the '60s? That ended the day he shipped me off to Haunt-Bourne's boot camp. You hear me? Don't come near her."

The man sighed.

"We're not the enemy, son. This is bigger than you. Bigger than her."

When Daddy noticed me in the doorway, he went pale.

"Go on, Ramey," he said softly. "Go to bed, baby girl."

I did. But I didn't sleep. Because that's when it hit me. Whatever they wanted. They couldn't say it by asking, and that's when they started planning to break me.

10

USE YOUR ILLUSION I

1991, seventh grade.

I'd come a long way from the misfit kid in that homemade dress.

But I still remembered that first day like it was burned into me.

I could see those girls clear as day—matching All Star basketball jackets, brand-name shoes—looking me over like they were deciding whether to laugh or spit. Dila was the ringleader. She cocked her head all polite-like.

"Cute dress," she said.

"Thanks," I beamed. "My mama made it."

They fell out laughing.

"Where'd you get those shoes?" one asked, snide as hell.

"I dunno... Kmart?"

More laughter.

I went home fuming.

"Mama, can I get me some brand-name shoes?"

"For what?" she snapped.

"Because the other kids have brand-name stuff! I'm the only kid in the whole school wearing home-sewn crap!"

She just huffed. "Oh come on, Ramey. It gives you character. Those girls don't have anything you don't have. I tell you what—next time we make a trip to Hancock Fabrics, you can pick any pattern you want. I'll sew it up with my cute little label—'Sew Good,' blue butterfly and all. There you go—brand name."

"And I don't appreciate that language, young lady. You are in the third grade now, almost nine years old, and dignified young ladies do not use such trashy words. You are my beautiful, smart daughter, and I make sacrifices so you can have nice things. Don't throw them back in my face."

"Why do you think I named you Ramey Victoria? Hmm? It stands for victorious, and that is what I expect from you. Those store-bought clothes will just make you blend in, and you, my angel baby, were not put on this earth to blend in. You are special. Therefore I'm going to need you to act like it."

And she was right.

By the end of that year, everyone and their grandma was paying her to make them M.C. Hammer pants.

She made me a pair in every color.

From laughing at me to paying me.

Cha-ching.

She even let me keep half the money.

And for once, I even made a new friend who wasn't a boy—back in middle school the year before. And none of us can forget how we got close. It started in the most craziest, horriblista ways.

Last day of elementary school—show-and-tell. Bring a pet or some particular item from home.

Mama was already lingering around the halls at school on the regular—changing out books across all the parish libraries, even the school programs—so she had her nose in my business enough. When show-and-tell came, Daddy was the one I called.

He loved it. Usually the only man there, strutting proud, sticking out like a sore thumb.

"Ramey, I tell ya what—I'll bring Damian!" he hollered over the phone.

I heard shuffling, then: "Damn it, Eric said he'd be damned to hell in a hand basket if I was gonna bring that snake and not him! Shut up, Eric—you can come. It's okay, huh?"

I couldn't tell if he was joking, but that rough laugh of his reassured me, briefly, he was just playin'.

It was the end of fifth grade, and the cliques were already carved in stone. Who was who and who wasn't—written across cafeteria tables and recess blacktops like gospel. The school system even started assigning seats, that's how thick the lines ran.

Me? I got stuck between Darlene Thibodeaux and Shawna Boudreaux. Both of 'em in band, both smart as hell, both quiet—at least at school.

We weren't friends, not yet. Not until show-and-tell.

Daddy strutted in proud as ever, tattoos still scabbing raw on his arms, eyes bright like he'd been up all night. High as a kite, he rolled my old baby carriage right through the door—his so-called "paddy wagon." And inside that carriage? Eric the Skull, propped up in a blanket like he was my baby brother, and Damian, the five-foot python draped heavy and restless.

Couldn't move, couldn't smile, couldn't do nothing but stare blank and wide—but in Daddy's mind, Eric and Damian were part of the family showcase.

For a second, I was flying high. My daddy, my snake, my skull—beat that.

Daddy knew Eric didn't talk to anybody but him. Said the skull did it on purpose, just to make him look a fool. So prankster he was, Daddy had a little recorder stashed in his pocket. Every now and then he'd click it, and out came these scratchy phrases—"Howdy, partner," or "Don't touch my eyes."

The kids thought it was weird, sure, but funny-weird.

"Your dad's so cool," they whispered.

For a second, I believed 'em.

Then Darlene's daddy walked in carrying a flying squirrel named Pecan. I think even Daddy said "awww" under his breath. Hell, the whole room did. That thing was a puffball with eyes, adorable enough to make even a python jealous.

And me? I sat there, proud of my weird shit one minute, embarrassed as fuck the next—

Darlene's daddy was younger. Clean-shaven. Fresh shirt, pressed jeans, neat hands. Made Daddy look wild—hair long, beard untrimmed, tattoos scrawling his arms like fresh wounds. My excitement soured fast. The heat climbed my cheeks till I felt red as a tomato.

But life don't bless sometimes without a sprinkle of cursing first.

Damian snapped Pecan up in one gulp.

Two little legs twitching in the air, then gone.

The room exploded. Girls shrieked, boys hollered, kids scrambling up desks like the floor was poison. Darlene's daddy cursed loud, and my daddy—standing there with his snake in one hand and his skull in the other—just muttered, "Instincts. That's all."

Teacher nearly fainted, flapping her arms like busted wings.

And me? I sank down small, proud and ashamed at the same time, watching the man I worshiped roll a skull and a snake into school like it was a carnival act, only to leave me holding the weight of a flying squirrel's last dance.

Still, even back then, I was already catching on. I'd seen how the big wigs in town could make a disaster look like a blessing, how the fixers fixed and the taskers tasked, patching over rot with a ribbon like nobody'd notice. They'd hand out miracles on the front porch while burying curses out back.

And maybe I wasn't in their league, but I understood the pattern.

If you can't undo the mess, you find a way to balance it.

That's the game.

My face burned hot, red as a tomato, heat climbing straight into my cheeks. I wanted to melt through the floor. Couldn't carry that kind of guilt—not even for a minute, much less all summer.

So before I slid back into my seat, I dropped down beside Darlene, hand shaky on her shoulder, scared to death but knowing I had to say something.

"Hey, Darlene... ya know last winter when it snowed that one day?"

She blinked up at me, eyes wide behind them coke-bottle glasses, and nodded.

"Well, that was me. I asked God for it, and... well, He did it. So... I been thinkin'. I can't give you your squirrel back, but if I pray real hard, maybe God'll fix your eyes so you don't have to wear those big glasses no more. They not cute—I'd hate it if I had to wear 'em. I mean, not sayin' you're not cute, just—oh fuck, shut up, shut up."

She just kinda nodded, not sure what to think, I'm sure, and it went quiet.

Didn't matter. I'd already decided.

I prayed all summer, every night.

I didn't know what I was supposed to be back then. Heads and preps. Combat boots one day, girly dress the next. I was figuring it out. My friends up the bayou were fancy. The ones down the bayou? Different vibe. You could smell it, feel it in the air.

Daddy said they were jealous. I didn't see why.

We were different. He wasn't like the other parents, and I wasn't like the other kids. And that couldn't have been more obvious to me when "Pharmacy Kathy" walked in to console her traumatized daughter, Darlene. Of course she was Darlene's mama—the secretary from the mental health clinic. She recognized me and Daddy right away.

So instead of waiting until bedtime to pray, I went ahead and got a head start—because if I couldn't balance the scale…

Kathy was younger than him, but she still was in the classroom that faithful day in '64. She knew he was mental, maybe even more than he knew about himself. And if the prayer didn't work, then I'd be canceled and confirmed crazy. I was trying so hard to avoid that label but here I was.

See, his friend Kathy worked at the mental health clinic. I'd been there with him a million times to pick up his meds. He'd nod in her direction and tell me stories:

"You see that lady right there?"

"Yes sir."

"Ask her about that nun that hit your Aunt Rue. Oh, she'll tell you."

Because she was there. We all went to Catholic school together—me, Kathy, your Aunt Rue.

"Oh yes, it's true," Kathy said. "Sister Clara had it in for Rue. Poor thing had epilepsy. Sometimes she'd say or do things that didn't come out right. Sister Clara acted like she was being a smart-ass on purpose, started beating her with her ruler.

"Levi wasn't even supposed to be there that day. But he showed up. He saw it happen. He grabbed Sister Clara by the habit and told her to stop. When she wouldn't, he stopped her himself. Broke her nose! Blood squirted everybody in the front row. I'll never forget that day," she continued.

I remember hearing that, thinking: Damn. My parents are nose breakers. And I thought that was so cool... but this situation?

NOT cool.

Truth is, I was a kind kid.

I respected people's feelings.

Maybe too much.

Maybe I was just soft.

Maybe I was a people pleaser.

Even then—when I was too soft, too naive, too much a child until I wasn't—the Rain Man came with the season. Summer's shine gone, replaced by cold, mean truths sharper than Mama's punishments. If I could reach that girl again, I'd tell her what the years finally taught me: nothing holds forever. Not silence. Not pain. Not even cold November rain.

11

Saltwater Knuckles

First day of sixth grade, bus pulls up, door hisses open, and there she is. No glasses. Eyes straight as the horizon. She runs up, wraps me in a hug so tight I almost fell over.

"We're best friends now," she said.

I laughed nervous, trying to shake her off just enough. Huggin's cool—as long as it don't drag on. Most girls were catty anyway, and if Darlene held me much longer, she might get ideas about playin' doctor. And Lord, I wasn't about to clock her eyes back crooked after I'd prayed 'em straight all summer.

"See? I told you. God listens to me. Don't always make sense, don't always come pretty, but He listens."

She tilted her head like she wasn't sure if I was bragging or confessing. So I doubled down, shit, it had worked so why not.

"I can't fix everything, Darlene. But if I can get'um to change the weather, or your eyes, maybe I can ask for bigger things too. Maybe that's why He made me so… weird. To notice the stuff nobody else asks Him about."

It landed quiet between us, not church-pretty, not rehearsed — just raw. And somehow, that was enough. She smiled and slid in the seat beside me, like she understood even if she couldn't explain it. That's how our friendship started — not with matching clothes or secrets swapped, but with me saying something half-crazy, half-holy, and her deciding it mattered anyway.

I wasn't a goodie-two-shoes but I really tried to be. Had the potential to be one of the "good, smart ones," I'm sure I coulda if I'd tried a little harder. But it's like I couldn't help it — the crazy would just leak out sideways. I cussed a lot for a kid. Not like I ever got away with it. I dropped the f' bomb, Mama dropped that right palm. Sometimes I wished I was normal, didn't say the wild shit that made grown folks gasp. But part of me liked it — my quiet revenge.

I was a clown at school, but I kept my grades up. Teachers liked me cause they could flex on me asking up so many questions.

I remember my first Black friend. Pierre. There weren't any Black folks "down the bayou," so the first time I saw him I was too damn excited.

"Pierre, can I touch your hand?"

"Why?"

"Well, my daddy said Black people had sticky hands. I wanna see if that's why Michael Jackson's always wearing that glove."

Teacher wrote a note home sayin' I'd made a racist statement. Mama was pissed. Daddy laughed so hard he about choked.

"I didn't say sticky hands! I said sticky fingers. They steal, Slick!"

Pierre was cool. Once he realized I wasn't racist, we became good friends, still close today.

I wasn't hard to get along with — just had my mouth sayin' dumb shit I didn't understand. Always crawlin' out of holes I made myself.

Those were the last days I still sounded like a child.

Didn't know it yet, but the world was already shifting under me —

one inch at a time.

And while I was busy tripping over my own mouth,

Daddy had started tripping over shadows.

He was acting stranger than usual— quieter, eyes scanning corners like something might crawl out. Muttering under his breath, then shaking his head like he's trying to clear static. Guns N' Roses had just dropped new cassettes, and we'd sit in the dark singing every word by candlelight while I read the booklet like scripture.

Maybe God tries to give you a heads-up before the wave hits… only thing is,
It can only help if you recognized the signals.

That's when the dreams started.

SALT WATER

"And in this corner, Salt Water Knuckles, going against the champ... Sir Fluffernox the Horned Horror!"

The room was dim, walls of steel and concrete closing in like a bunker built for the end of the world. I looked down—my hands were pink, plush, and round. A teddy bear suit. Soft, ridiculous... and mine.

A roar cut through the silence. Out of the shadows shuffled a monster—half muppet, half nightmare, its felt skin ripped in places, foam stuffing and feathers spewing out like guts. Its eyes were stitched-on buttons that rolled wildly, and its mouth—just black cloth—snapping open and shut as it lunged for me.

I swung, my padded fists landing with a dull thud. It wasn't enough. The thing knocked me back, claws ripping at the fake fur on my arms. I stumbled, ears ringing inside the ridiculous over-sized teddy bear head, trying to keep balance as it closed in for the kill.

Then I saw him. Daddy.

He was across the room, locked in his own fight with a fat man in a pinstripe suit, the kind you'd see in an old gangster film. Daddy moved fast, desperate, but the man grinned—a gold tooth flashing—and in one smooth motion, leveled a gun.

The shot echoed like it came from everywhere at once.

Pow.

Daddy's head snapped back and—God—just came off, rolling into the shadows like a lost toy.

I screamed, but no sound came out. Tried to wake up, tried to move, I was paralyzed.

Finally I bolted upright in bed, drenched in sweat, the phantom feeling of that teddy bear suit, knarly puppet feathers still clinging to me like a second skin.

Something in me tugged. I didn't know why — just that something felt wrong, different.

I called his house early. No answer.

12

USE YOUR ILLUSION II

Meanwhile, on the Other Side of the Parish Somewhere between the Pharmacy and Le Guêpe territory, a war between two worlds was coming to a head.

I still wonder what was running through Daddy's mind that night. I wasn't there. Wouldn't know most of it till years later. But I know what he wasn't thinking.

If he'd known what leaving me like that would do—would he have done it anyway?

Did he think it would soften the blow, all those "just-in-case" funeral drills? "Yes, Daddy, I know your song. Pocket tee and jeans, no suit, and a joint." I know now you were trying to prepare me in the only broken way you knew how—even while something in you was slipping loose.

Gawwwd, you could've never imagined what it would carve out me.

That your little girl—the one who worshiped the cracked

floor you walked on—would learn to call volatility love, and insanity home.

That the way you burned would become the only map I'd ever trust.

That I'd grow up with nothing but a busted Quiet Thing, a devastating drug habit, and a life spent chasing fallen things and back road demons looking for the man who once called me beautiful inside his hell.

I don't think you ever could've really known what this would turn me into, Daddy.

Maybe you weren't lost in thought at all. Maybe you were carrying out the only plan your unraveling mind could still hold—driving because stopping meant facing the thing already eating you alive.

I can see the truck rattled through St. Faux, engine coughing, static whispering your name. October air heavy as regret. Bonfire smoke crawling over the cane fields. Mulberry candles taking the place of jack-o'-lanterns. You pull into the pharmacy lot, headlights dulling like they didn't even wanna witness.

Inside the cab, your jaw was locked tight, sweat slicking your temples. Eric ridin' shotgun, patient and quiet.

Nobody told me right away what really happened—that you'd gone back to the Gep's house in the middle of the night. She was your grandma. She'd raised you.

They said she heard someone at the kitchen window—barely a foot high above the sink, near impossible to crawl through. I can picture you there, thin and shaking, the night holding its breath.

She woke up, grabbed her shotgun, aimed it steady. Said she couldn't be sure who it was. Said they ran off into the dark.

But you knew. And you couldn't run far enough from what you'd gone there to find.

Folks whispered their versions after—pawn-shop lies and porch-swing theories. Said you were desperate. Said crack had hollowed you out. Said you were looking for money, pills, mercy, anything.

But I know better now. Or maybe I just know differently.

I can almost see you behind the wheel, staring straight ahead while Eric's skull sat grinning on the dash.

"No, Levi... do not proceed," Eric says, voice glitching in soft mechanical hums. "Government threat level: nonexistent. We are a unit. We operate as one system. Purpose: light. Directive: protect Levi. Maintain alignment with the thousand-star protocol."

Daddy, did you hear him? Did you hear Eric trying to save you? Did you hear me too? I was calling you, Daddy. I was calling you all day.

You wipe your face, breath catching. "Uh-uh, Eric. They'll have to find somebody else to be their next Oswald."

"You know Oswald? They started with him at twelve—locked him up, called him disturbed, taught him how to shoot. Sent him overseas, rewrote his head, made him useful. By twenty-four he's a ghost with a rifle. That's the pattern, Eric. Take boys with no home and make 'em into headlines."

You stare through the windshield, voice down to a hum. "Ain't no Manchurian candidate left in me. They already rewired the whole circuit."

You sit there a while, sweating, trying to find the man you used to be.

Inside, the lights are too bright. The bell rings sharp as judgment.

Kathy's behind the counter—your old friend from the Catholic school days, back when you were the kind of boy who'd punch a nun for hitting his sister.

She tries to smile. "Levi," she says,"Picking up your prescription?"

You nod, drop Sunny May's damp bills on the counter. Your hand shakes.

She looks a moment too long. "Take care of yourself, okay?"

You walk out fast, the bell shrieking behind you. Climb into the truck. The pharmacy bag rattles beside Eric.

Eric's voice cracks like a radio losing frequency. "Please, Levi… go home."

You shake your head. "Home's gone."

Your hands grip the wheel so hard your knuckles split open, blood gathering in the grooves. The radio's dead, but the static keeps talking.

Then maybe—just maybe—you hear it, clear as a name whispered through the wires:

I am the Angel of Death.

You slam the dial, but the voice keeps crawling.

End it, Levi.

You're shaking now, trying to remember why you came. The bag in your lap feels heavy as sin—five bottles inside, enough to silence the noise for good.

You think about Sunny May's hands pressing that money into yours. About the Gep's shotgun, steady in the dark. About Kathy's soft voice—*Take care of yourself, okay?*

And then you think about me.

That's the part that burns the worst.

You open the bag, thumb trembling over the cap. Eric's glass eyes gleam blue in the dash light.

And I can almost hear you, low and tired, that half-gone grin in your voice—

"Maw Sunny paid for your funeral..."

You pause, eyes on the E.R.I.C.

"...guess she paid for yours too, ol' friend."

Daddy, I wish I could've been there. I wish I could've stopped you. I wish I could've told you that you didn't have to carry it all alone.

I wish I could've told you that I loved you. That I still love you. That I'll always love you.

But you ain't gave me the chance.

13

Is This Real Life?

I never missed school. Five years of perfect attendance, and not 'cause I wanted it—Mama demanded it. So when she let me stay home without a fight? That should've been the first red flag.

I spent half the day calling Daddy's house, aggravating Uncle Vincent who had just recently moved in. Every time I rang, he gave me the same gruff answer:

"Your dad's sleeping and I am too. I beat on the door a million times. He won't get up. I got work tonight, so stop wakin' me up, cher."

Click.

I stared at the idiot box, fork draggin' through my plate, but my gut was louder than the TV—it already knew somethin' was up. Daddy never went three days without calling me. Didn't matter if he was out of town, doped up, broke, sick—he always called.

So I called Aunt Rue. She lived next door—Buzz's mama.

"Hey, Aunt Rue, it's me. You seen Daddy? He hasn't called in days. I'm getting worried."

Her voice tightened. "No, baby. His truck's still out front. I'll walk over and try to wake him up."

"Well ya know how hard he sleeps. If he don't answer, break in, do somethin'! Please. I just need to know he's alright."

"Don't worry. I'll call you right back."

But an hour dragged by. No call. No nothing.

Where the hell is everybody?

That's when Mama screeched into Maw Sunny's driveway. She came in wailing, mascara streaked down her cheeks. One look and I knew.

My stomach already knew.

"I'm so sorry," she said.

The moment I'd dreaded my whole life unrolled right there on Maw Sunny's linoleum. I wanted her to tell me something different. Anything but the truth my bones already carried.

"Cousin Jasmine found him," she whispered. "Your Daddy's gone."

"No!" My throat tore.

I bolted for the bathroom, soft drink spewing from my nose like a geyser. I gagged, heaved, tried to breathe through the flood.

I can't live without him. I can't.

I begged to see him. Mama resisted. Said it wasn't a good idea. Said the coroner was already there. Said the room was sealed.

I stormed out anyway. She followed, finally agreed to drive.

I cried the whole ride. My damn soul leaking out in streams down my face.

We turned onto his street. Detectives were pulling away, their tail lights smearing red. Only one car lingered.

Buck sat on the trunk, face buried in his hands.

When I jumped from the van, he ran to stop me. I broke free, screaming.

I kicked through relatives, hands pawing at me with their useless words—

He's in a better place. It was just his time.

Shut up.

I tried to push through the door. Tried to get to him. But Buck blocked me.

"Ramey, no. You don't want to see him like that."

"I need to," I sobbed. "I **need** to."

He shook his head, eyes red. "You don't. Trust me."

But I could smell him.

It was faint at first—like something sour left too long in the sun. Then it hit full: sweet rot, copper, and something sharp like mildew and old pennies. The kind of smell that clings to your throat and makes your stomach turn before your mind catches up.

That smell of death.

It curled around the porch like it was looking for me.

And it found me.

I collapsed against the porch rail, fists pounding wood. Jasmine wrapped me up, held me while I broke down into something less than human.

Then Buck knelt beside me. Pulled something from out his briefcase. Held it out with both hands like it was sacred.

It was a blood-stained 8×10, my second-grade school picture. The one I hated. One of Mama's Sew Good dresses, crooked collar, big cheesin' grin, my gapped front teeth showing proud.

Buck said it was still clutched in both hands, arms straight out above his head. Like maybe it was the last thing he saw.

I took it, hands trembling.

I didn't get to see him. Didn't get to say goodbye. But I saw this. And it carved me just the same.

Mama came to me then, guilt pouring off her like sweat.

"Hit me," she said.

"What?"

"Hit me. It's my fault. Hit me."

I stared at her, numb.

"Is that what you do?" I asked.

Her face fell.

Grief had stripped the mercy clean out of me.

And even then, in that moment innocence got peeled off skin from bone, I couldn't punch my mama.

Innocence,...

Once it's gone, you finally get it—why rebels rage. Not 'cause they wanna burn the world down. 'Cause the world already burned them. And rage is the only thing left to keep the ashes warm.

Scripture says: *My eyes fail from weeping, my heart poured out on the ground.* (Lamentations 2:11)

Yeah. That's about right.

Grief don't just bend you—it spills you wide open in front of everybody, and the dirt don't give it back.

And right there in that dirt, I swore my vow.

If I ever got blessed with children, I'd bleed before I made them bleed.

Folks say don't make promises like that—too crooked a world to keep 'em. Maybe so. But I carved it in bone that night, and bone don't forget.

Is this real life?

I asked myself that over and over.

But grief don't answer questions. It only echoes—rippling back like a tidal wave of other things.

14

Halloween October 31,1991

Daddy's funeral was packed,
wall-to-wall with faces I didn't even know half the names of.
It was held at St. Lazarus of the Lost Cause—
the same place Mama used to drag me to on holidays
when she was trying to prove we were "good people."
He was laid out in a dark green casket—
the exact color of Eric's war helmet.
I'd picked it out myself,
figuring he'd appreciate that kind of army nod.
Truth is,
I climbed right into that thing at the funeral home,
testing how it felt before they put him in it.
The Gep about lost her religion right there,
arm skin flappin' as she snatched me out like I'd just cursed at Mass.
"Get outta there, girl! You gon' wake the dead!"
"Bless your heart," I mumbled,
knowing I'd near gave her a heart attack.
Daddy had brought me and my new friends to the fair not too long before that.
Moose had introduced me to them,
and they all came out to support me that day—

even if they spent half the service
plotting to steal the money out the collection tray,
and making out with Darlene in the cemetery.
After the 21-gun salute,
an Army vet stepped up and handed me Daddy's folded American flag.
I clutched it tight,
sobbing so hard my nose ran like an old faucet.
Uncle Lucian and Uncle Buzz—
Aunt Rue's husband—
slid Daddy into the mausoleum
while I stood there holding that flag like it could keep me upright.
And then I did the only thing that made sense to me—
I put on his song.
"And at my grave you stand,
just say God's called home... your Ramblin' Man."
That was Daddy's send-off.
No fancy speeches,
no angel choir—
just Hank Williams Sr. singing our truth while I cried like a baby.
Everybody said he was "sick,"
like it excused the rest.
But I couldn't quit thinking—
if God made him that way,
would He cut him some slack,
or close the gates just the same?
—
Uncle Lucian and I looked around the house,
gathering Daddy's stuff.
I walked over to his collection of hats on the bookshelf.
Empty prescription bottles clattered to the floor
as I pulled down a cowboy hat.
I called my uncle over,
and he'd stumbled onto something even stranger.

After setting a fan in the window to drive the sour stench of death from the room, he knelt and dragged a pillowcase from beneath the bed. It was knotted shut with an old extension cord, swollen and heavy in his hands.

When he loosened the knot,
sharp edges pushed against the cloth.
I leaned in—
then gasped.
It was Eric.
Busted ceramic.
Blue doll eye still staring through the tear in the fabric.
My chest caved in.
Why would Daddy do that to him?
Why seal him away like trash
when he'd sworn Eric was family?
After Daddy's funeral,
I decided Eric needed one too.
Didn't matter he was just shards and plaster dust—
he was ours.
I picked up his pieces
and laid them in a shoebox
I'd lined with a scrap of red velvet
from one of Mama's old dresses.
Jasmine stood with her hands clasped like a preacher,
and Buzz came barrelin' up holding something on a paper plate.
"Look what I found," Buzz said,
wide-eyed.
"It's a frog.
He's dead,
but not like regular dead—
he's flat dead."
Jasmine gagged.
"That's gross."
"He was on the road," Buzz explained matter-of-fact.

"A car made him into… like, two frogs,
but still one frog,
you know?
He deserves respect."
"Fine," I sighed.
"Put him next to Eric."
We stood in a row by the china berry tree.
Jasmine cleared her throat like she was about to marry somebody.
"Eric was a good skull," she said.
"He didn't scare nobody,
except that one time Buzz screamed and dropped his ice cream."
"That was not fear," Buzz protested.
"That was a jump scare,
and I only screamed because y'all rigged him to fall off the shelf with fishin' line."
I smirked.
"Maybe,
but it was still funny."
Buzz ignored me and turned to the frog.
"He hopped good till he didn't."
Jasmine's tone got serious,
like she was speakin' to the frog's kinfolk.
"If the frog family is listening nearby,
I just want y'all to know…
he died a hero,
crossing the road in broad daylight.
Y'all should be proud."
Buzz nodded.
"And he didn't even get flattened for nothin'.
We're givin' him a proper service."
Jasmine glanced toward The Gep's house,
then whispered,
"We should have communion."

"What are we gonna use?" I asked.
"Bread," she said,
already walking toward the fence line like it was settled.
Five minutes later,
we were back with half a loaf of The Gep's French bread,
a Dixie cup of grape Kool-Aid,
and the kind of guilt you can only get
from robbing your own blood kin.
We tore the bread into chunks,
dipped them in the Kool-Aid,
and declared it holy.
Buzz went first,
then Jasmine,
then me.
That's when we heard it—
the sputter and roar of The Gep's riding lawnmower.
She came around the corner like a wasp in full flight,
hollerin',
"Y'all think I don't see my bread in your nasty little hands?!"
Buzz tried to hide his piece under the frog's paper plate.
Jasmine stuffed hers in her mouth whole and almost choked.
I just froze like a deer in headlights holding my Kool-Aid like a communion cup.
The Gep dropped the mower into high gear and came after us,
weaving across the yard like she was herdin' cattle.
We scattered—
me with the shoebox,
Buzz still salutin' the frog, like it was Veterans Day.
Jasmine over there tryin' to finish chewin' before she got caught.
We didn't stop running
until we were back under the china berry tree,
breathless,
with the bread safe in the dirt by Eric and the frog.

Jasmine wiped her mouth and said,
"Well,
at least they got communion before The Gep murdered us."
Buzz shrugged.
"Worth it."
We hummed Amazing Grace,
off-key and out of breath.
When it was done,
Buzz whispered,
"Rest in pieces…
but in a nice way."
We covered the box and the plate,
patted the dirt,
and stood back like we'd just done somethin' real important.
Maybe we had.
—
It took two whole years for me to realize
my father was never coming back.
In that time,
I mourned him religiously
every single day.
I would dress up in his torn-up jeans and pocket T-shirts
and place his hat on my head,
pretending it was him standing before me in the mirror.
For a year,
I kept his scent of alcohol and cigarettes
sealed in a plastic zipper bag.
Every day I sniffed the bag
until the scent was gone.
I held séances,
hoping to talk to my daddy on the other side.
Mama was a librarian,
so I spent a lot of my life in libraries all over the parish.

I read everything I could get my hands on—
astral projection,
life after death,
how to conjure up dead relatives.
I read the Bible, too.
I even bought a Ouija board.
Mama had to get holy water
because weird things started happenin' in our house.
Lookin' back,
I was getting pretty dark about it all.
I got more morbid trying to reach him
and started cutting myself.
I actually liked it back then.
Thinking about it now,
it's just so dark.
But that was just the start of it.
Losing Daddy tore a hole in me
that never really closed.
Mama stopped beating my ass so bad after his death—
that was probably the only good thing come out of it.
I think she realized
beating me into submission
wasn't working quite like she expected.
She even tried to buy me some new clothes
so I'd fit in better at school.
But it was too late.
I was already the weirdo kid
who talked to ghosts
and smelled like cigarettes and grief.
And if I thought I had it bad living with Mama before,
I was still so damn naïve.
By fifteen,
I'd be packing a bag

and leaving home for good—
just praying anything
would be better
than what I was about to go through.

15

Lookin' for Daddy

After the funeral, I thought the worst part would be missing Daddy. Turns out the worst part was how quiet it got. Just me and my thoughts. If I questioned everything before he left out, I had a million gazillion more. Just me, stuck with Mama, and I already knew better than to ask her.

By then, Mama had done graduated from bank teller to parish librarian, taking any college class she could. Woman stayed in classes like she was allergic to free time. She'd come home smellin' like chalk

dust and self-righteousness.

If I didn't understand somethin', she wouldn't give me the answer. Nope. She'd plop twelve Websters

right on my bed and say, "Look it up, dear — it builds character."

That fucker.

I'd glare at her and say, "I know you know the answer, woman."

And she'd grin, proud as a cat.

"Yeah, damn right I do. Know how? I looked it up."

Mama was always hard on me about my grades.

She'd say, "A smart girl don't waste her brain bein' lazy."

Well, I didn't waste my brain or my time.

I sat between two of the smartest girls in class —

didn't even have to study, just listen close and write fast.

Hell, half the time I cheated off 'em
and still scored higher than both of' em come-state test at year's end.
Sleep quit me cold turkey.
It's like something had died in me too.
Not just Daddy — me.

I'd lay there all night,
jaw clenched,
cryin' into the dark.
"Why'd You take him, Lord?
Whaa whaa."
Mama filled the house with books—
psychology, psychiatry,
anything that made her feel like it could fix me.
Every week she diagnosed me with somethin' new.
"I think you're depressed, Ramey."
Next week:
"Maybe it's bipolar disorder."
Week after that:
"Could be schizophrenia… like your daddy."
I'd come home to a new medical book.

Then one day Mama came home real proud of herself,
like she'd finally found the missing screw in my soul.
She said she'd been talkin' to Kathy—
Darlene's mama—
Dr. Reimann's still there," she told me,
voice lifting like hope had just walked through the door.
"You remember him, right? He treated your daddy.
Says he's taking new patients now."
And where was he from?
"You remember Haunt-bourne Medical & Mental Sciences Campus?"
"Oh, you mean the nuthouse?" I said.

"Yeah, I remember that place."
Mama frowned like she'd tasted vinegar.
"It's not a nuthouse, Ramey.
It's a treatment facility."
"Yeah," I said,
"that's what Daddy called it too—
right before they treated the last bit of sense outta him."

In the waiting room, there was a little candle in a red glass cup,
one of them Catholic-looking ones
that ain't got no saint on it
and still feels watched.
It didn't flicker like flame—
it pulsed, slow,
like a throat swallowing.
I remember thinking:
if you put a candle in a storm cellar,
it don't turn the cellar into a church.
It just makes the spiders easier to see.
And if you stare long enough,
you start wondering
who lit it in the first place.
When I came in for intake,
I expected—I dunno—
a clipboard maybe?
A stethoscope?
Instead, one of those relics in a lab coat,
face carved up like a rite of passage,
rolled in with a box on wheels

big enough to make a coffin nervous.
"What's that?" I asked.
"Your chart," he said, calm as rain.
"Hi Ramey, remember me?
"Not really," I admitted.
He let out a soft little hum,
like a mechanic listenin' to an engine
and liking the sound.
"Alright," he said.
"Everything's still where it belongs."

My God father used to say
a man can carry his sins in his hands
or he can hide 'em in a trunk—
either way,
he still gon' smell like it.
That box on wheels rolled in
like a trunk with manners.
And I thought about how some folks don't bury bodies—
they archive 'em.
They put a number on the forehead
and call it mercy.
A coffin got a lid.
A file don't.
A file just keeps on eatin' itself.

CASELINE_1977-0047 * H4UN7B0RN3PR0J3C7-7UMBL3W33D

"Well, damn," I muttered.
"I didn't say that much in intake
What y'all do—call up Jesus for a reference?"
He smiled polite—
the kind of smile that hides a thousand screams—
and pushed the box against the wall.
My stomach dropped.
How the hell they got that much on me
when all I gave was my name and birthday?
Daddy's voice crawled up out the back of my skull—
that half-laugh, half-warning he saved for when shit was about to get real.
"The doc said I'm crazy, Slick.
*Shit—**you** gonna be too*
once they pump you full of them psychedelics.
You'll start readin' code through the walls,
seein' all the little demons changin' things—
history, future, the parts they don't want nobody rememberin'.
Doctors ain't right in the head neither.
You gotta be half-possessed to do the things they do in the name of science.
And listen here—
even if you are crazy,
don't you ever let 'em know what's really goin' on in that mind of yours.
Ain't their damn business.
Tell 'em only what you want 'em to know."
So I did.
I wasn't about to be bipolar—
that felt like the kind of crazy folks crossed the street to avoid.
And I sure as hell wasn't gonna try to act schizophrenic like Daddy—
I didn't have that kind of stamina
or that kind of death wish.
But I'd read enough books
and memorized enough symptoms

to play the '90s manic-depression victim to its limits.
'Cause in the '90s, everybody knew one thing:
the Manics got the good prescriptions.

It wasn't hard to figure out how to get what I wanted— Doctors liked to feel smart, like they were saving you from yourself.

All I had to do was cry a little, talk about Daddy, and they'd scribble out a prescription like they were handing me a lifeline.

Mama didn't ask questions, just handed me the pills and told me to be quiet.

And the kids at school? They were even easier. A few tears, a few stories about my dead daddy, and they'd give me their lunch money, their snacks, their secrets.

I thought I was in control, thought I was the one pulling the strings. But the truth was, I was just a puppet, dancing to the tune of the pills and the pain.

That was the bridge I didn't mean to cross—
but hell, once they hand you the bottle,
you're already halfway over.

Pills couldn't fill the void Daddy left—
But hey I knew what to do....

16

Side Effects May Include: Shadow Trippin'

I'd look it up.

That's how it started — the experiments, the visions, the idea that maybe I could reach Daddy another way.

I spent hours in Mama's library, readin' about seances, astral projection, and how to talk to the dead.

Mama was a Catechism teacher,
babysittin' me at church
like I was her student.
I bucked hard.
Changed religion out of spite.
She followed me there too,
sat in the back row and grinned like she'd won.
Next thing I knew she'd shipped me to Bible camp
like it was court-ordered.
That night before she sent me off,
I had set up my first séance.
I spread Daddy's pocket tee across my bed like an altar cloth.
Lit every candle we owned.
Set the Ouija board on top.

Pressed my fingers to the planchette and whispered,
"Daddy… are you here?"
The damn thing twitched.
A cold breeze whipped across my face—
no windows open,
no fan running.
A candle popped,
dripped thick wax onto Mama's green shag carpet.
That's when she burst in.
"What in God's name are you doing, Ramey?!"
"I'm talking to Daddy!" I cried.
"Heathen!
You don't play with dead spirits!"
She stomped every candle out
With her man shoe size 12 stomp jumping foot!
Daddy used to call Mama a stomp jumper, cause was from North Louisiana.
Wax flying everywhere,
grabbed the Ouija board like it might bite her.
"You wanna talk to your daddy?
Go to church!"
She packed my bag by dawn.

At camp, I woke cold.
Something low moved across the room,
fast as a rat—
but shaped like a man's shadow.
I pulled Daddy's shirt from my pillowcase and whispered,
"Please… just be you."
But deep down, I knew better.

A seam opened in the dark,
slipped shut before I could blink.
Brother Thibodeaux's silhouette filled the doorway.
"Child, you feel that?" he whispered.
His eyes went past me—
like he recognized an old trespasser.
He ushered me to the chapel,
sat me on the front pew,
laid his work-worn hand over Daddy's shirt.
The prayer pressed in—
low and river-strong—
until the shadow backed off
like a dog that knew the boot was comin'.
You're safe now.
I didn't feel safer.
I hadn't felt unsafe to begin with.
Just... **seen.**
I wasn't just looking for Daddy.
I was opening doors I didn't know how to close.
By then, I'd stopped being a girl who missed her daddy.
I'd become a girl willing to talk to shadows.
And that kind of girl?
She was bound to find trouble.

On weekends,
I ran wild with Moose and Darlene.
One day I showed him my prescriptions,
flippin' through the labels like it was a party trick.
He squinted,

tapped one.
"Slick,
says alcohol may intensify the effect."
Well,
shit.
We took that as a challenge.
Next thing you know,
we're raiding every cabinet in St. Faux Parish.
Blood-pressure pills,
expired cough syrup,
somethin' that might've been for gout—
we didn't care.
I was 13, bored, and dumb enough to meet the devil halfway.
And when one of them mystery pills hit juuust right,
I slapped the counter and said,
"Man, y'all gotta try these—

The Great Dry Socket Revival of '94

We'd been chasin' God
through every bad idea St. Faux Parish had to offer,
and that night He showed up wearin' Darlene's fuzzy top hat.
Looked like it belonged on the lady from that Cranberries video, *Zombie,*
if she'd joined a carnival cult.
Darlene was sittin' cross-legged on the floor,
Crazy-ass hat pulled over her face.
"Aw,
shit," I said,
"She's in there hidin'."
Moose fell over laughin' so hard
he near aspirated a cigarette butt.
We'd been on that cheap LSD—
the kind that made ceiling fans talk in parables.
Somewhere around midnight,

Darlene declared she could see sound,
and Moose swore the roaches were line-dancin' down the hall.

By dawn,
the trip had dissolved into what I now call
The Great Dry Socket Incident of '94.
I'd had all four wisdom teeth yanked the day before
and was doped up like an injured mule.
I called the doctor,
slurrin' through my swollen jaw.
"Doc,
them pills ain't workin'.
I ate 'em all.
I need more."
He said,
"I prescribed thirty!"
I said,
"Well,
I prescribed pain,
and here we are."
So there I was—
jaw thumpin' like a bass drum,
head beepin' like a microwave on the fritz.
Darlene came over with hot beer
she'd bought with a forged note from her grandma
and sympathy smokes.
Said we'd ride the pain out together.
We rode it straight into a stupor—

The socket might've been dry,
but the humor wasn't.
My cheeks went to swelling a little.
Then came the mushrooms.

Moose had picked 'em right out the cow shit—
claimed you could tell the good ones 'cause the cow'd been lookin' philosophical.
Me and Darlene ate ours and waited for enlightenment.
Instead,
the blanket we were sittin' on
started levitatin' like it wanted outta this world too.
I looked in the mirror and—
swear to God—
I was a lion:
Fresh spiral permed mane,
frizzy and fro'ed.
eyes swollen damn near shut.
Fat *Matou* face.
Darlene beside me looked like some elegant egret
with eyeliner and daddy issues.
Moose walked in,
saw us both mid-hallucination,
and said,
"Y'all look like the goddamn food chain."
That's when I realized—
maybe we were:
predator,
prey,
and whatever the hell Moose was,
all orbitin' the same lunacy.
I laughed so hard I felt my stitches pop.
Blood,
smoke,
and revelation everywhere.
By the second night,
my whole head was so swollen
I was afraid it'd pop.

The gauze had quit hours ago—
blood and spit makin' a little pond in my lap.
Darlene was in the corner under that enormous fuzzy hat,
rockin' like a gospel singer at her own funeral.
I hollered,
"Girl,
what you doin' under there?
You prayin' or hidin'?"
"Prayin'."
"Really?"
So I got down on my knees
and tried to look up in the hat with her.
Now,
logic says I couldn't have fit—
but painkillers and psilocybin said otherwise.
Somehow I was in that hat—
all of me—
lookin' around like a tourist in Hades.
"Aw hell,

Darlene," I said,
"it's nice in here!
Little hot,
though.
Smells good—
like teen spirit.
Whatcha prayin'—
oh,
never mind."
She'd tipped the Sindoppler—
that last beer—

and damned her eyes back crossed,
like two drunks meetin' at a four-way stop.
"Come on,
Ramey," she said.
"Help me pray again,
like you did that summer."
I told her,
"Uh-uh.
You seen my face,
Darlene?
I can't face the Lord lookin' like the goddamn Elephant Man.
I can't even whistle right now.
My jaw's broke,
my face buzzin',
and if the Lord sees me like this,
He's liable to smite me just for symmetry.
You go 'head and open the prayer line;
I'll join in when the swellin' goes down."
Moose was laughin' so hard he nearly passed out.
The beer tipped,
the ashtray flipped,
and we both tumbled out from under that hat
like two sinners fallin' outta grace.
By sunrise,
the smokes were gone,
the air reeked of cheap perfume and bad theology,
and my jaw was hummin' like a nest of hornets.
Darlene was still wearin' that hat.
Moose was facedown on my algebra book.
And me?
I was halfway convinced the Lord had been watchin' the whole time—
takin' notes and laughin' His divine behind off.
The next day,

the joke quit bein' funny.
By noon
my face had turned the color of shrimp boil—
the socket festerin' and the fever climbin'.

Right before Mama busted in,
the room dipped cold—
not AC cold,
but grave-yard-door-left-open cold.
A shadow peeled up the wall behind Darlene,
tall, crooked,
head cocked like it recognized me
from some other nightmare.
It wasn't Daddy—
I knew that bone-deep.
It moved like the same thing
that stalked him in his worst days,
the one he'd stare past me to see.
Darlene must've felt it too—
her eyes went crossed and glassy,
and she yanked that big fuzzy hat
down over her whole damn face again.
like she could hide from somethin'
that didn't need eyes to find her.
The shadow leaned in,
close enough I felt it thinkin' about takin' one of us.
I whispered,
"I see you.
You ain't takin' me."
Didn't matter if it heard—
I heard me.
And right when it bent low,
like it was choosin' which soul to snatch—

Mama stepped through the doorway.
The thing snapped out of the room so fast
the air popped like a rubber band.
Mama didn't see it straight on,
but she damn sure felt the tail end of it—
her eyes darted to the corner,
sharp as a woman who's caught evil before.
That's when she looked at me and said,
"Sweet Jesus, girl—
you're goin' to the ER."

Turned out it wasn't just dry socket.
It was a full-blown infection—
and appendicitis on top of it.
The doctor said,
"You're lucky you came in when you did."
I said,
"You're lucky I didn't eat all your pills."
They cut me open,
packed me with gauze,
and gave me morphine strong enough to make angels hum.
Somewhere between the beeps of that heart monitor,
I swear I heard Darlene's voice echo through my head:
"Come on,
Ramey.
Help me pray again."
And I did.

17

My First Potential GTA

I was fourteen the first time I almost got charged with grand theft auto.

Mama was still strict as shit back then, tight as a jar lid you couldn't twist off no matter how hard you tried.

If I wanted to breathe a little, I'd slip over to Maw Sunny's for the weekend.

Part of it was 'cause I loved her—she'd let me yap her head off all night, noddin' like every word mattered.

But the other part? Maw Sunny would slide me them little pony beers behind Mama's back, grinnin' like it was our secret gospel.

So that night, it was just me and her, drinkin' quiet in the kitchen till the clock stumbled past three.

Just enough to make me feel bold, like the world couldn't catch me even if it tried.

That's when I picked up the phone and called Lob, still buzzin' from the ponies and the idea that maybe—just maybe—I was grown.

Darlene was always braggin' about stealin' her daddy's truck since she was twelve, like it was a family tradition.

I figured, *How hard can it be?*

Didn't even bother with shoes.

Just a pair of cutoff Girbaud jeans, a pink Duck Head collared shirt, and my hair yanked into a sloppy ponytail.

Barefoot on the pedals, I got Maw Sunny's minivan started and pointed it toward his house like I knew what I was doin'.

Except I didn't.

Well shit, I hadn't thought about how I might needa know what buttons to press to see how fast I was goin', but I'd just crack the door a little and catch the speedometer glowin' by the parking light—like that was a good idea in Golden Meadow, Louisiana, the speed-trap capital of the world.

Sure enough, blue lights lit up behind me.

One cop car at first.

Then two.

By the time I decided to "lose them," there were four cruisers on my tail, sirens wailin' like the whole parish was in on the chase.

I floored it—if you can call it that in a stolen Maw-Maw minivan with a drunk kid at the wheel—dartin' down side streets until I hit a dead end.

Gravel crunched under the tires as I stopped.

When I turned my head, I was starin' at gun barrels and flashlight beams.

I stepped out, still barefoot, still buzzin', hands up like I'd seen on TV.

They freaked out when they saw I was just a kid.

A drunk, laughin' kid.

That's when the genius in me kicked in.

See, I was slick like that—always tryin' to unfuck myself in the dumbest way possible.

I dropped to my knees and started scoopin' up handfuls of wet ditch mud—shovin' it in my mouth. Then I heard Daddy's voice: "Lord have mercy, girl… You eatin' mud. The only thing left is to start barkin'."

The cops shouted, "What the hell's she doin'?"

One of 'em said, "She's eatin' it—she's eatin' the mud?!"

They thought I was hidin' drugs in my mouth, when really I was just tryin' to get the beer smell off my breath.

I must've looked like a rabid possum in acid-washed jeans, crawlin' around, snortin' up mud water and swearin' I was fine.

They backed off like I was contagious.

One radioed for backup, the other kept his flashlight trained on me like I might sprout fangs.

Finally one said, "Hell, just let her mama deal with it."

Turns out, they knew my family, of course.

Golden Meadow's small like that.

Instead of haulin' me off, they let me call *someone* to come get me.

Even better, I called my aunt, figurin' if i asked polite enough she'd keep it between us.

By the time my aunt showed up, I wasn't even a suspect no more—I was company. I was sittin' behind that little desk at the station like I belonged there, barefoot with my feet kicked up and crossed, wearin' one of their hats like I wasn't the reason we was all there. The police was huddled up around me, laughin' and leanin' in while I ran my mouth and told stories like we was at a fish fry. We was cuttin' up, havin' us a good old time, and I swear I forgot why we was even havin' this little get-together—till my aunt walked in and reality pulled a *kick-doe,* like a lick gone wrong.

"Slick, I'm gon' tell you right now... any chance of you lookin' sane is over. Might as well lean into it now."

If you gon' be a fool, at least be a legendary one. 'Cause if ya Mama don't kill you... "the parish gon' talk about this till Jesus come back." Pahaa.

She showed up all sweet, talkin' to the officers, smilin' like everything was fine.

But when Mama walked in behind her?

She didn't fuss.

Didn't scream.

Didn't say much of anything.

Just looked at me—me standin' there barefoot, reekin' of ditch water, smilin' up at her with my mud-lit grin.

That silence hit harder than any belt ever did.

Like she'd given up, lost the cause.

I felt played, embarrassed, and worse than anything—guilty.

So I did what any stupid fourteen-year-old in that kind of trouble would do.

I drank two bottles of NyQuil.

The green kind.

When I woke up, my head was heavy and the world was tiltin', but I was alive.

Just hallucinatin', sweatin' through my sheets, still half-drunk on NyQuil and bad choices.

Sad to say, it'd take a lot more than that lil baby brush with the law for me to realize I wasn't immortal.

Back then I figured I was untouchable—
just a barefoot outlaw with a hangover and a fresh second chance,
grinnin' through the wreckage,
bayou-proof and flashin' that mudlight smirk.

18

The Misfit 5

I still visited as often as I could my godparents on daddys' side.

They weren't nearly as watchful as mama. Truth was, they let me do whatever the hell I wanted. I'm sure I drove 'em nuts—raiding their pantry, leaving Little Debbie graveyards on the counter. My Uncle Buzz was a quiet man. Never fussed. Just grunted, flipped the empty snack boxes over, and that grunt was my cue to slip out the door and hit the streets and end up at Mooses' place.

By fifteen, I was Slick—Daddy's nickname for me. A "diamond in the rough," folks called me. Sun-bleached blond hair, green eyes sharp enough to cut glass. Strangers said I was pretty, family teased I'd break hearts one day. I wished I could see it. All I saw was bait—hooks buried in every compliment. Pretty didn't feel like praise. Pretty felt like a setup.

I wasn't settin' trends. One week preppy, next week grunge, mostly flannel and combat boots. fashion didn't matter. I didn't need a boyfriend—I had my boys.

First up: Ace, a.k.a. Moose. Still chubby, red-headed, clever in that dangerous way kids get when nobody ever tells 'em no. His window was a fake ID drive-thru—Polaroid camera, borrowed laminator humming like a lawnmower. Five bucks and you could be twenty-one with a dead uncle's birthday. He called it harmless fun. We knew better. Moose wasn't just playing with matches—he was huggin' the whole can of lighter fluid.

Next up, Chalk Line Charlie. After "The Indian Outlaw[16]"—a student chasing pro-fighter dreams—knocked him out cold one afternoon. He hit the floor so clean it looked like somebody had traced him in chalk, arms and legs splayed out like a crime scene outline. The name stuck, less insult than legend.

He was a goofy bastard, legs made out of boiled noodles. We spent half our teen years in his pool room, smoke curling up while his parents were gone, laughter bouncing off the walls like we were untouchable. Chalky wore the nickname like a badge, grinning under the brim, "He sucker punched me. Anyway, he threw up like a girl when he saw the blood," as if being remembered for the way you fell was better than not being remembered at all.

"Oh, the blood from your jaw he yeeted across the bayou? The one we all watched spin like a bottle rocket before somebody went to collect the remains?"

Up next, but look down. Lambard Beauragaurd, A.K.A. Lob. A short, pudge-nerl & ADHD tornado—bouncing off walls, everybody's favorite chaos goblin. "Lob wasn't the plan; Lob was the interruption. The kind of interruption who could turn a traffic cone, a Pringles can, or a busted trombone into a working bong before you finished asking how. "Gravity never caught him, and neither did the rules."

And Sam, a.k.a. Shawz

Our weed plug, our doorway into every bar in town. Mullet and Converse straight out of an '80s VHS tape, like he'd stepped out of a grainy rental copy and never updated the look. He named us the Misfit Five—without him, we'd just be four dumbasses with no weed.

He even fronted his own screaming band, veins bulging, throat shredded, microphone clutched like it was the only thing keeping him alive. I could never understand a single word he screeched about—lyrics melted into static—but that was the point. He wasn't singing for sense. He was singing for release, for the chaos, for the thrill of being louder than the world.

Offstage, he was the one who could talk his way past bouncers, bartenders, and cops like he'd been born with a backstage pass. One minute we were broke kids with fake IDs, the next we were leaning against sticky bar counters, smoke curling up, drinks in hand, like we owned the place.

He was the hinge of the crew—the one who kept the doors open, the joints lit, the chaos humming. If the Misfit five were a band, Shawz was both the front man and the plug: screaming into the void, then slipping us into places we had no business being in.

The first day of high school came for everybody else. Not us. Possumpalooza was the same damn day, and we weren't missing it.

That morning, I snuck a little red, white, and blue bikini under my school clothes—my ode to secret freedom. Grabbed my bag, jogged out to my ride: the shit-brown, oversized van I called the Great Mama-Jama. My first wheels. My curse. Every time I complained, Mama said the same thing:

"It gives you character."

"Oh Mom, none of the other kids wear hand-sewn clothes. Can I get something brand name?"

"No. It will give you character."

"Can I play sports?"

"No. Read a book. It'll give you character."

"Can I get a real haircut?"

"No. Split ends will give you character."

Character, character, character. My life was one long punishment disguised as a personality trait.

I rolled my eyes, fired up the beast, adjusted the cracked Kurt Cobain mirror dangler, and threw it in gear. The horn croaked like a dying moose as I picked up the rest of the M.f.s. Smoke rolled out the sliding door as they piled in like circus clowns.

"Everybody got their tickets?" Moose asked.

"Hell yeah!" Shawz grinned.

"Our parents are gonna kill us," Lob said, sparking a joint.

"Not mine," Chalky shrugged. "They're shrimpin'. Won't be home to rat me out."

"Shit," Moose muttered. "Don't matter where I end up, long as I'm outta my mom's hair."

"Yo, Shawz," Moose drawled, "pass around those scorpion hits."

Shawz dug in his pocket, smirking. "Already on it." Handed over a square of paper stamped with a blue scorpion.

"What the hell are scorpion hits?" I squinted.

"Dude," Shawz's eyes lit up. "It's acid from this old hippie. Best batch in years. Pop it. We're about to go on a delusional mission, way the hell out the box."

I stared at the little square. *This is gonna get me out the box?* I thought. Then I popped it in my mouth, chewed, swallowed.

Thing about Moose—you couldn't tell him nothin'. This wasn't his first brush with infamy. Couple weeks before, he convinced Darlene's kid brother, Little Nicky—who everybody called Roach Clip 'cause he couldn't finish a joint to save his life—to climb the water tower by St. faux High.

"I just wanna see the parish from God's angle," Moose said.

Only problem was, God didn't build no stairs on that tower. They got halfway up, started hollerin' about the view, then realized the ladder ended before the top.

Next thing you know, whole damn fire department's out there, Channel 4 News circlin' in a helicopter. Roach Clip's up there waving like he's in a parade pissing in it and Moose is hollerin', "Don't drop me! My mama'll kill me before I hit the ground!"

When they got 'em down, the fire chief just shook his head. "Y'all gonna give Jesus a nervous breakdown."

Roach Clip's mama grounded him for eternity, Darlene got roped into guilt by association, and Moose got suspended again. The parish was on boil alert for a month due to contamination. By the time Possumpalooza rolled around, he was local famous. Folks at the gate were pointing like he was Elvis.

"Hey, that's the Water Tower Boy!" somebody yelled.

Moose grinned, gave 'em a peace sign, and I swear right then I should've known—wherever Moose went, rescue crews weren't far behind.

By the time we hit the gates, the acid slapped me sideways. Colors buzzed, the world glittered, my stomach fluttered like a trapped bird. I felt like I was floating.

"Do you feel it?" I asked Chalky.

"I don't know, but I feel something," he mumbled.

Shawz rolled on the ground laughing.

"You feel it?" he asked, kicking his legs, makin' fun of me.

"You're stupid," I said, and kicked him in his chur[17]!

Then Moose bolted for the trees without a word.

"Where you going?" I hollered.

No answer. So we chased him. High as hell, lost him in the crowd, until we spotted him—stuck way up in a tree. Of course.

"Moose! Get down!" I shouted.

He hollered back, "I had it but I lost it!"

A crowd gathered. Moose was up there, red-headed sideshow, hamming it up. Then a damn news crew showed. The cameraman leaned in:

"We're live at Possumpalooza, where firefighters are attempting to rescue a young man stuck in a tree."

Firefighters finally dragged Moose down, his big ass dangling from the ladder like a hog strung up for market. Soon as his feet hit the ground, the air shifted. When they hauled Moose out the tree, this sharp sulfur stink hit me—perm solution mixed with firecrackers. For a second I thought the firefighters had singed his drawers on the way down.

That's when **Rob Reck News** shoved a mic in his face.

"Moose, do you have anything to say to the rescuers?"

He wiped his forehead, blinked hard, and said, "Ya damn right I do… I had it, but I lost it."

The anchor leaned in. "Well… what is it?"

Moose squared his shoulders like he was about to deliver scripture. "It is yourself," he said, "an' you gotta face it."

And Lord help me, that made more sense than I'd ever realized.

Before the crowd scattered, Darlene popped up beside me, all eyeliner and craziness, grinning with a Coke in her hand. "Happy birthday, Slick," she shouted over the amps. "You only turn fifteen once!"

The stage roared to life. August 18th, 1994. University of New Orleans soccer field. Smashing Pumpkins[18] headlining, sun bleeding into the horizon. The heat was biblical.

When *Today* hit, the acid turned liquid in my veins. Darlene and I pushed forward into the pit, laughing until the laughter broke. Somebody shoved.

The crowd surged. My ribs folded. Darlene's hand slipped from mine.

Then what I'ma just call—the undertow. Dust, screaming, sound warping into light. I went under.

A hand found my arm. Calloused, steady. Then another on Darlene. An angel fell from the sky with black curls and eyes like he'd been born staring down hurricanes.

"You girls tryin' to die or what?" he said, with the cutest dimpled face I'd ever seen.

That was Orion, "The Indian Outlaw". He pulled us clear of the madness, dropped us by the fence, and the world came back slow—one heartbeat, one breath, one guitar riff at a time.

Later, Darlene swore she saw halos in the smoke. I just remember thinking maybe being born again don't always come with holy water. Sometimes it's sweat, distortion, and the wrong boy's hand pulling you back to life.

Sure enough, my stepdad caught it all on the local news that night.

That's why Daddy called me Slick—not because I was slick enough to get away with shit. I never got away with a damn thing. I was always caught. Mama swore she felt it in her bones when I was up to no good. And sure as shit, she always busted me.

Daddy's rule was simple: "Deny till you die. You don't owe nobody nothing."

So I tried.

"That's crazy. Must be a coincidence. Maybe my friends were on TV, but that girl wasn't me."

Didn't matter. Mama knew. Mama always knew. Like the universe had given her front-row tickets to every mistake I ever made.

19

The Indian Outlaw

It was a hot sack of Satan summer afternoon. A disturbance was brewing in the Gulf of Mexico, but this time it wasn't Mother Nature's fault.

After checking and baiting over two hundred crab traps, I sat at the bow of the narrow ten-foot skiff and lit a cigarette. Dried fish scales stuck to my fingers, and bits of rotten chum clung to my ponytail.

For four summers straight, Chalk Line Charlie and I had been running some of his stepdad's crab traps to earn spending money. And every single summer ended the same: Chalk Line Charlie stayed fresh and clean while I ended up muddy, stinky, and cussing.

See, I had to run all the crab traps myself—'cause even though I was rough and tough and could outwork half the boys, I was still me.

And according to Mama, I couldn't find my way out a wet paper bag.

She'd say, "Ramey, you could get lost on your way to the front porch."

And she wasn't wrong—I flipped or wrecked just about anything I tried to drive. So driving the boat was never an option.

Our haul that day was pathetic. Two hundred traps and only one crate half-filled with crabs—about sixty dollars' worth.

And just when I thought the day couldn't get worse, Chalk Line Charlie dumped the whole box overboard and fell ass-first in the bait.

That's how we got here.

"Sit there and soak, Chalky. Maybe that pokey funk'll finally baptize the bullshit outta you," I snapped.

He reached in, grabbed a nasty little bait fish, and fired it like a bullet.

It hit my left cheek and stuck.

Didn't flop. Didn't fall. Just oozed down my face like it knew it had a job to do.

Chalk Line Charlie howled laughing.

Bad move, brotha.

I peeled that sucker off slow, face blank, already gone to war in my head.

Then I launched.

I crossed that boat from bow to stern like my feet never even touched the crates. Skipped right over 'em like some deranged swamp ballerina and came down on him with my lil fists of fury.

"OKAY, Mighty Midget—I'm sorry, calm down!" he shouted, still laughing, arms flailing like a man already halfway drowned.

Chalky's fat ass was still stuck in the bait box, flailing like a turtle on its back, while I was peelaying him with everything I had.

Pick! Pack! Pick! Pack!

We didn't always fight out on the water. Sometimes we had no choice but to work together.

There was this one time—we were broke as hell and out of smoke.

Daddy used to say, "No dope, no hope."

And dammit, he wasn't wrong.

So we gathered our traps and headed out anyway, desperate for hope.

At the boat launch, everyone was in a frenzy—tying down, yelling, pulling out. A few old timers hollered at us to turn around.

I guess they knew something we didn't.

Because not five minutes out, the sky cracked open. A Louisiana storm dropped down like the wrath of God. Thunder. Wind. The kind of rain that stings your skin.

And just like that—the whole damn engine flipped out the boat.

There we were, drifting in a busted-up skiff, waves slapping the hull, everything soaked and scattered.

I stood up like some wild-ass Cajun Lieutenant Dan, one leg bent behind me, arms raised, pointing to the sky just like in the movie—

"IS THAT ALL YOU GOT?!"

Me and Chalky must've watched Forrest Gump[19] a million times.

And there I was, dead serious, channeling Dan in the middle of a hurricane.

Lightning struck the marsh so close I felt the hair on my neck rise.

"God damn, Slick!" Chalky shouted.

"You always saying crazy shit—shut the fuck up and help me with this damn engine!"

I was mid-prayer when Chalky let out this Hulk scream—face beet red like it was about to blow the hell up—and somehow, he muscled that engine back into the boat.

We managed to drift to an old camp dock and hid out under the porch until the storm passed.

I guess that's why they were yelling for us to turn around.

But we never did listen.

And here I was again, stinking like a rotting catfish in July, with fish guts in my brassiere.

It was Orion—the same guy who saved me at Possumpalooza, when I was high off my ass.

I looked like the Gulf itself had thrown me up for disrespecting it.

I wanted to crawl inside a crab trap and never come out.

As his boat eased closer, I tried to calm myself, but it was too late.

Orion took one look and shook his head.

“Man, you really let a girl beat you into a corner? What the hell’s wrong with you?” he hollered.

“I didn’t let her! I fell in!” Chalky snapped back.

“Even worse,” Orion teased.

“Who you got there with ya?” Orion called.

“You don’t know her? My little slave!” Chalky laughed, pressing my last nerve.

I whipped around with a half-smile that was anything but friendly.

“This clumsy motherfucker just dumped my entire day’s work overboard, then got his ass stuck in the bait. And since he can’t shut up, I tried to shut him up for him. Matter of fact, if you don’t mind, I’m jumping in with you. Let this stupid shit get himself unstuck.”

Orion cracked a grin.

“I think that’s a great idea. Hop in. I’ll take you home. Don’t worry, Chalky—I’ll yank you out before we leave.”

I climbed into Orion's boat without another word and stomped into the cabin to wash up.

Once free from the box, Chalky pulled Orion aside.

"Look, man—she's pissed at me right now, but she's like my little sister. I know you. Don't even think about trying anything."

Orion raised an eyebrow.

"Yeah? Didn't I split your eyebrow open already?"

Chalky rolled his eyes.

"Yeah. Then you ran to the bathroom and puked like a little bitch. I mean it—try something, and I'll burn your house down."

Orion just smirked.

"Whatever, man."

He climbed back into the boat and handed me a towel.

"So ya finally taking me up on my offer?" Orion teased.

"What offer?" I asked, still scrubbing fish guts off my arms.

"All school year I tried to give you a ride home, but your dumb Misfit five buddies kept cock-blocking me," Orion said.

I snorted.

"We come from different worlds. Besides, I feel pretty stupid standing here covered in mud."

"Don't feel stupid," Orion said.

"I think it's badass that a pretty girl like you knows how to work these waters. I've seen you checking traps out here a million times. You really know what you're doing."

"Better than flipping burgers at Burger Hut," I shrugged.

"Wanna grab a bite before I take you home?" Orion asked.

"I'd like to, but Chalky lost today's profit. I'm broke," I admitted.

"Don't even worry about it. I got you covered."

I paused, then cracked a crooked smile.

"Maybe next time I'll pay if we end up like this again."

I probably shouldn't have spoke that into existence—'cause bae bae, I'd pay for it alright.

And in my gut, I knew I would.

20

Daiquiris, Drag Queens & The Death Curse

It was my first date.

It wouldn't be the last,

but it was the one that set the tone for the majority of my life.

He was older—eighteen, cool, already a little dangerous.

The kind of boy you know you should run from but can't help but chase.

He had a buddy with him, and the buddy had a girlfriend my age, Kristy.

The four of us thought we were grown.

We were wild, unsupervised, and riding through the streets of New Orleans like we owned them.

We stopped for daiquiris—because that's what you do in New Orleans when you want to feel grown.

And like every good story in my life,

it started with a drink.

That's one of the last clear memories I have from that night.

The daiquiris.

The Quarter.

Them saying, *"Damn, these drinks are strong huh, girls?"*

—fuck yeah they were.

Turns out later we found out why.

They'd slipped Quaaludes in them.

Looking back, that was really fucked up.

And at the same time—knowing me back then?

Hell, he didn't even have to lie about it.

He could've said, *"Hey Ramey, I got some bad ass date-rape drugs, want one?"*

And I'd probably have said, *"Awe shit, give me two."*

If something felt dangerous, I ran straight toward it.

Next thing I know, I'm sitting in Orleans Parish Prison filling out a police report.

Not for getting jumped by some mugger in an alley—nah.

By a whole damn squad of drag queens.

Last thing I remember clear as day was some big ol' tall bitch in six-inch heels with a man grip like a vise.

Then—poof—nothing.

Next thing I'm blinking at the fluorescent lights in OPP going:

Well, damn... how the fuck did that slip my mind?

"Man, baby girl—you slammed that first one down," they said.

"But we was outnumbered."

Can't believe it.

Really got jumped by a whole damn pack of drag queens.

Hell, I ain't even mad about it.

Wrong place, wrong time.

Trying to play grown in a world that'll swallow you whole.

But for real though…

where'd that time go?

They had backup.

A whole crew.

We were outnumbered and got jumped, dragged, and left bleeding in the middle of the french Quarter.

But the night wasn't over.

After that, I came to again—my face stuck to his windshield.

Literally stuck—blood dried in my hair, my head glued to the glass.

I peeled myself off and looked around.

We had crashed into a light pole.

I was in the front seat, alone up there, bleeding and foggy.

The boy and Kristy were passed out in the back, heads slumped together like rag dolls.

Well, that would've never worked with us all sleeping like that. Somebody got to drive.

The pole was halfway across the hood.

I didn't even know who'd been driving when we hit it.

Nobody did.

So Kristy and I went looking for help—barefoot, bloody, and stumbling through the Ninth Ward.

We finally found a little corner store with bars on the windows.

Now mind you—it was 1995.

Bars on windows wasn't even a thing back then,

'less you were selling crack or hoarding scratch-offs.

It was scarier than a gator in a porta-potty.

The clerk didn't want to let us in—two teenage girls looking crazy at two in the morning. But when I turned and said," Oh look Kristy, its ok they got the car started."

...and they sped up instead of stopping, just left us standing there—bloody, stranded, and looking ridiculous in the middle of the road.

Eventually the clerk cracked, unlocked the door, and let us in. and we called Kristy's daddy.

He drove over an hour and a half to come get us.

That should've been the end of it.

But it wasn't.

When we finally got home and went to the hospital, I found out I had a concussion.

No surprise.

But the real kicker came later.

Turns out, the guys—the ones who were supposed to be looking out for us—

had spent the rest of that night wrecking cars, stealing tires, wandering

train tracks…
not even realizing they'd left us bleeding in the street.
My mama forbid me from ever seeing him again.
So naturally, a month later,
I moved in with him.
Bless his heart—he didn't know it yet.
Shit, I didn't either.
But he'd seal his fate with his seed.
That's a whole other story.
(And one hell of a curse.)

21

Cut From Asshole to Appetite

I remember how brave for no reason I felt.

I'd been sneakin' cigarettes all summer,
and Mama had this thing
where she'd sniff my fingers the second I came in the door.
To see if they smelled like smoke.
Well, I was sick of that shit.
She was standin' at the stove,
sweat rollin' off her brow, stirrin' her pot.
I wasn't hidin' it no more.
I walked right in, took a long drag off my cigarette,
and let the screen door bang behind me.
"Mama, I just wanted to let you know—I smoke cigarettes now,"
I said real calm.
"You don't need to sniff me up no more. I just wanted to get that out the way."
She didn't even turn around at first.
"What you said?"
"You heard me," I huffed. "I smoke. Yeah."
Next thing I know—
pick, pack, whack, smack.
She wiped her brow with the back of her hand

and went right back to stirrin' that pot.
"Now you don't," she said.

The ends justify the means,
that's what she'd always said.
But that's only if the means work.
She tried so damn hard
to make me into something respectable.
But the day I told her I was movin' out?
She didn't holler.
Didn't flinch.
Just stood there lookin' at me
like I was already halfway gone.
And maybe I was.
I knew she pitied me.
She, felt guilty, too.
I used it.
Leveraged every ounce of it to get my freedom.
I promised myself I was gonna show her.
I'd prove I could do better.
Make her proud.
Orion made that too easy.
It was only a matter of time before I fell for him
after the accident.
And honestly?
The more Mama hated him for leavin' me in New Orleans that night,
the more I wanted him.
Is that all it took to get her attention?
Get a boyfriend?
Funny how some folks gotta watch you bleed
before they even blink.
With Orion, I didn't have to be scared of her anymore.
He cheered me on every time I pushed her buttons.

I stayed gone for nights at a time—
didn't care.
Why go home when someone else would love me instead?
But deep down, I was hopin' it would fix things
between me and Mama.
Maybe they'd get along.
Maybe she'd finally see I was worthy of love.
Yeah...
that backfired.
"Where the hell you been?" she barked.
"Well, if you'd just pick up the phone and call Orion's house,
maybe you'd know," I snapped back.
Her palm cracked across my face so hard, I hit the floor.
I clutched my cheek, eyes locked on her.
"I'm sick and tired of your shit," she spat.
"This is my house. And you're not welcome in it anymore.
Get out."
"What?"
"You heard me. Now get the hell out before I throw you out myself."
I got up slow. Tremblin'.
Orion walked in right on cue.
"Everything okay in here?" he asked, clueless.
"No, Orion, it's not," she snapped.
"You and her have made my life miserable.
I never want to see either of you again."
Orion looked stunned.
"Come on, Ramey," he said.
"Get your stuff. You can stay with us."
I turned to go to my room,
but Mama grabbed my arm,
ripped open the door,
and shoved me onto the porch.
I fell hip-first on the concrete.

Scraped my palms bloody.
Orion ran to help me.
"She don't have anything here anymore," Mama hissed.
"Everything in that room is mine."
Orion squared up.
"You're crazy. I'll never let her see you again—even if you beg."
She laughed, mean and hollow.
"You're just a kid. You'll dump her soon enough.
And then she'll come crawlin' back.
But I won't be here to help her."
Orion pulled me close.
"We're gonna get married.
We're gonna have a baby.
And you'll never see your grandchild.
As far as we're concerned, you don't exist."
Married?
A baby?
I blinked at him, stunned.
Orion hustled me to the car.
"What am I gonna do?" I whispered.
"You're gonna stay with me.
You'll never have to go back there again," he promised.
"That's what I'm scared of," I said soft.
"She's the only parent I got left.
I don't wanna be an orphan."
"Don't say that. It'll work out."
Five months later.
Three months pregnant.
We moved into Aunt Rue's old house
next door to Daddy's.
Yellow siding.
Three bedrooms.
Gorgeous old wood floors.

I felt like a princess.
Scrubbed walls, cooked Orion breakfast,
rubbed his back, ran his bath—
never asked for a thing.
But the ache stayed where my mama should've been.
She didn't come to the baby shower.
Wouldn't speak to me.
Maw Sunny tried to play peacemaker.
But I couldn't face her.
Labor was hell.
"Hi Ramey, how are you?"
"Great! We're ready to induce!"
"Prep me?"
Fleet enema and a shave."
Lord have mercy.
At seventeen,
that was the last thing I wanted Orion to see.
But I survived it.
Then came the contractions.
"This fuckin' hurts—don't TOUCH me!"
"You're five centimeters. Want the epidural?"
"I WANT THE EPIDURAL!"
Didn't last.
Pushin' felt like bein' split in two.
"I'm shittin' on myself!"
"No honey, the baby's head is out!"
Maw Sunny peeked in
just as the doctor made the cut.
"Ohhhhh shit!" she hollered.
"They done cut ya from asshole to appetite!"
I wanted to die.
Then the baby was out.
Orion laughed at my hemorrhoids.

"Looks like triplets tryin' to make their way out."
"Shut up and look somewhere else!"
He held up the placenta like it was a science project.
"Uh, Doc? Hate to scare you,
but I think you took out one of her organs."
"Orion! Stop playin' with that! You makin' me nervous!"

First days home were what you'd expect.
Feedings every two hours.
Diaper changes.
No sleep.
I cried in the dark
while Orion snored like a sawmill.
Two weeks in, Orion's parents offered to take the baby
so we could rest.
Orion had other plans.
"Let's go out."
"I just wanna nap."
"That's all you ever want. You lazy."
I snapped.
"Todd's mama lives next door and helps them every day."
"Whatever. I'm dressed. Let's go."
We went barhoppin'.
Did coke.
Two weeks after givin' birth,
I was wired and exhausted,
staring at the ceiling at 6 a.m.
I whispered into the dark:
"Hey God, it's me.

I know I ain't talked to you in a while.
I feel so alone. So crazy.
Please help me.
If you make this feelin' go away,
I swear I'll never do this shit again."
Forty-five minutes later,
I was back at it.
Lesson learned?
Hell no.
I just got used to it.

22

Forsaken

By the time spring rolled around,
Orion and I had turned into two different species:
I was a nocturnal possum mama,
clutchin' her baby in one hand
and a cigarette in the other.
He was a Mardi Gras peacock—
colorful, loud, and always disappearin' when it mattered most.
I tried to focus on our baby boy.
Tried to get my head straight.
Maybe go back to school,
maybe even college one day.
But the truth?
The drugs were startin' to make more decisions than I was.
Dreams don't survive long on the bayou
when you're broke,
heartbroken,
and doin' lines off the back of a Blind Melon CD.
Orion had turned nineteen
and morphed into some kind of club-hoppin',
ecstasy-chompin' legend in his own damn mind.
I kept waitin' for the version of him who once said:

"I'll take care of you forever."

But that version got lost somewhere between the strip club and Candy's apartment.

Late one night, the phone rang.
Little Orie was crawlin' around
tryin' to eat lint.
I picked up the phone hopin' for love,
but got static and lies instead.
"Hey. My boss needs me to work extra.
I'll be home in the morning."
"Right. And pigs just flew past the window with timecards."
Click.
Frustration boiled up.
I ripped the phone from the wall,
marched out the door,
and flung it like a discus into the dark.
Po lil Orie justa lookin at me like,
"You done?"
Found him moments later,
headfirst in the trash can
like a miniature Oscar the Grouch.
I pulled him out and hugged him like the world was endin'.
Then I sat on my daddy's old porch
and started prayin' to ghosts.
That house, that driveway—
my heartbreak had GPS
and always rerouted me back to Daddy.
Five years gone,
and I still felt like I was waitin' for him to show up and say:
"You good, Slick?"
I whispered up to the stars:
"Are you here, Dad?
'Cause I'm about to lose it."

After the baby fell asleep,
I did what I always did
when I felt like a raccoon trapped
in a Dollar General dumpster—
I called Shawz.
Shawz was a walkin' contradiction:
had an Environmental Science book open
while he racked up lines big enough to ski on.
He answered mid-snort.
"Mrs. Betty Crocker! What's crackin'?"
"Man… I need a break from this planet."
"Be there in ten."
Ten turned into forty-five
'cause his grandma wouldn't shut up about Bingo—
but when he got there,
he came bearin' powdered gifts.
We used his Blind Melon CD—
'cause of course we did—
and cut lines thick as my disillusionment.
I took a big one and instantly regretted it.
Burned like hellfire,
then hit my stomach like a brick of guilt.
I puked in the sink
while Shawz cackled like a haunted jukebox.
"Good shit, huh?!"
"Let's call it… effective," I said, wipin' my mouth.
The baby started cryin',
and I danced him down the hallway
like everything wasn't fallin' apart behind the scenes.
Shawz gave him a head pat
and left me with a baggie of leftovers
and two Virginia Slims.
Later that night,

I did a few more bumps
and played ball with my baby
while hallucinatin'
that the kitchen tiles were tryin' to give me advice.
Meanwhile, Orion was starin' in his own B-movie—
down in New Orleans
hittin' up a strip club with Marc and Donny.
The place had more glitter than dignity
and dancers with wigs older than me.
Candy invited them to her place
for a post-show chemical buffet.
Orion didn't hesitate.
Back at home,
mornin' hit like a fryin' pan to the soul.
I was comin' down hard,
cryin',
feedin' cereal to a baby
who kept lookin' at me like,
"Why you sad, Mama?"
Orion finally showed up,
kissed the baby,
and walked back out like I was the babysitter.
I stood there with a cellophane bag in my pocket
and a heart that felt like roadkill.
He had gotten me disowned,
knocked up,
and now he'd ghosted me
with all the charm of a fart in church.
I had no money.
No help.
No plan.
Eventually, I called Maw Sunny for rides
and swallowed my pride like a bad pill.

One day at the store,
I ran into one of Orion's relatives
who offered me a job.
It wasn't what I wanted.
But it paid in cash.
And it was walkin' distance
from Orion's mama's house.
So I took it.
Gut a few nutria rats for a livin'?
I could handle that.
And somewhere deep inside,
I think I knew this was just the beginnin'
of the real war.
The one where I'd have to rescue myself.
Not from Orion.
Not from dope.
But from the part of me
that thought this was all I deserved.
Because when you're born in a swamp,
the only way out
is to crawl through it.
And I was just gettin' started.

23

Blood, Guts, and GED Dreams

3:33 a.m. Monday mornin'. Alarm went off like a jail siren. I slapped it quiet and lay there a second, breathin' deep. First day on the new job.

Maw Sunny had agreed to drive me until I could get on my feet. I threw on some old Z. Cavariccis and a T-shirt, bundled Orie up in his blanket, and hustled out the door.

We dropped him at Orion's mama Joy's house. Joy took him without a fuss. Maw Sunny and I didn't talk much on the ride. She knew I was nervous.

The nutria shed was older than dirt and smelled worse. Blood and guts caked on the walls. Floor slippery with God-knows-what.

First job was tackin' the hides onto boards to dry. Your hands went numb stretchin' 'em tight. Then they'd toss 'em in big-ass dryers. They came out inside-out, and my job was to flip 'em right-side again.

Five cents a board. So I learned fast.

But that was just the warm-up. Afternoons brought truckloads of dead nutrias to gut.

My boss Pop was an old Cajun fella with a handlebar mustache, big ol' round belly, and a whiskey laugh.

Everyone called him Pop. He was fair— but he didn't sugarcoat nothin'.

"Here ya go, cher," he said, handin' me a yellow slicker and gloves. "Think you can handle it?"

I forced a grin. "I guess we 'bout to find out."

He gave me a filet knife. "Pick one up and put it on the table."

That first carcass was a monster. Three feet long. Teeth like a devil's.

I nearly dropped it tryin' to heave it onto the table. Pop just laughed. "Cut her open and clean out everything but the bones."

The smell? Like the inside of a grave.

I gagged so hard Pop wiped tears from his eyes laughin'.

"You'll get used to it," he said.

And I did. Eventually. I even started flingin' intestines to the pelicans hangin' around. Pop would pass with his whiskey bottle, offer me a pull. Just enough to kill the gag reflex.

At day's end, I peeled off the slicker, rinsed the gore off my arms, and Pop handed me a crumpled wad of cash: **$97.10**

I didn't even care I smelled like roadkill. I had money in my pocket.

I walked barefoot up to Joy's house. Forgot clean clothes.

"Lord, child," she said, wrinklin' her nose. "Come in before you scare the neighbors. Here—take these clothes for the ride home."

"Thanks for watchin' him," I said. "I'll wash these and bring them back."

"Anytime. You know that," Joy said softly.

At home, I set Orie down. Normally we'd bathe together, but I was too filthy even for that.

Then I heard a knock.

"Hey! You gonna let me in or what?" Selma hollered before I even got the door open.

I grinned. "Get in here, you ol' fool. Been too long."

Selma was an old family friend. Used to be a knockout blonde. Now she was a tough, raspy-voiced brunette with a million miles on her.

She sniffed the air. Made a face. "Damn girl. What is that smell? Like somethin' crawled up your butt and died."

I laughed. "First day guttin' nutria. Didn't know what I was signin' up for."

She nodded, serious for a sec. "You and that boy done for good?"

"Yeah." I sighed. "I guess I always knew it."

Selma shrugged. "Shit, honey. That's life. But you're tough. You'll figure it out."

"Yeah, if I'm lucky I'll end up with a house full of pet rats."

Selma cackled. "Girl, I didn't gut animals for a livin', but I did suck a few old man balls for rent. Same difference—either way, you're up to your elbows in somethin' nasty."

I lost it laughin'. "Go shower. You're about to make the baby cry from the smell. I'll watch him."

By the time I finished, Orie was tucked in tight.

"Feel better?" Selma asked.

"Clean, anyway," I muttered. "Still guttin' rodents for a livin', though."

She gave me a look. "Better than nothin', babe. You're doin' what you gotta do."

We sat up half the night. Talkin', laughin', cryin'.

When nutria season ended, I had to find somethin' else. Didn't have many options. But I wasn't about to lay down and die.

I even pulled cement for six months. Back-breakin' work. Hot as hell too. But it paid that hundred bucks a day—cash in hand.

That was real money back then. Hell, that was everything to me.

Problem was... those jobs wanted to break your back and leave you smellin' like death. But they paid.

And as far as I was concerned, guttin' swamp rats was still a hell of a lot more dignified than baggin' groceries for minimum wage and fake smiles.

I might've been young, broke, and bruised— but I wasn't stupid. I had one rule: If I'm gonna suffer, at least let me get paid in cash.

So when Dollar Bougee called? I hesitated. Told myself this was somethin' clean. Somethin' respectable.

But deep down? I knew it was Dollar Bougee.

The only "store" in town where the roaches pay rent. Where the lights flicker like a horror movie trailer and every aisle smells like expired Pine-Sol.

Their motto? "Welcome to Dollar Bougee—where our prices ain't cheap, our air-conditioning don't work, and our ice cream sandwiches been thawed and refroze nine times since Clinton was president."

They sold shampoo that foamed like pancake batter, pickles that glowed in the dark, and lingerie so flammable it came with a lighter.

Kids traded baseball cards out front, but half the time they were prison mugshots.

You didn't shop at Dollar Bougee— you survived it, like a carnival ride with tetanus shots at the exit.

I told myself it was better than guttin' rodents. But honestly? At least the nutria didn't pretend to be somethin' they wasn't.

24

The Wrong Kind of Rescue

When Orion left, it wasn't just heartbreak.

It was a gut-punch that knocked the wind clean out my ribs.

I was loyal. Too loyal.

When I said forever, I meant it.

When he said, *"I ain't ready to settle,"* it felt like the world was telling me, *"You ain't worth settling for."*

And something cracked.

Not the loud kind of crack, like glass breaking.

A quiet one. Inside.

The kind you can walk around with for years, smiling, pretending you're whole.

That's when Bubba-Ray showed up.

Not on a white horse.

Not with flowers.

But with a cigarette hanging out his mouth, a gun in his glovebox, and eyes that said he'd kill for me if I asked.

That wasn't rescue.

That was ransom.

And I was the damn prize.

He played the role easy.

Buy me dinner.

Pick me up from work.
Whisper sweet nothings that smelled like whiskey and Marlboro Reds.
And me?
I let him.
Because it felt good to be wanted, even if it was the wrong kind of want.
But rescue's a lie.
There's no saving in it.
Only trading.
You trade one kind of pain for another.
One cage for another.
One leash for another.
I thought I was being rescued.
Really, I was just being recruited.
Pulled into his chaos, his hustles, his temper.
Bubba-Ray wasn't Orion.
He wasn't gentle, wasn't careful.
He was firecrackers in a gas can.
And I lit the fuse every time I climbed in his passenger seat.
Bar fights, motel rooms, back-road deals.
The man could turn a Tuesday into a war zone.
And me? I'd be there swinging too.
Not because I liked to fight—
but because I didn't know how to walk away.
Loyalty's a blessing till it turns into a curse.
And mine? It always turned.
Looking back, I know the truth:
I never loved another man the way I loved Orion.
Not Bubba.
Not the ones after him.
Every man after that was just convenience—
a ride, a roof, a warm body when the nights got too long.
Rescue turned to routine.
Routine turned to survival.

And survival don't look like love.
But here's the part I didn't see yet:
Bubba wasn't the devil.
He was just the errand boy.
A pawn in a game I hadn't learned the rules to.
The real devils wore suits. Smelled like cologne.
Sat at oak desks and signed papers that moved lives like chess pieces.
Compared to them, Bubba was just noise.
A distraction.
And I was dumb enough to think he was the whole storm.
Maybe that's the cruelest part.
You think you're getting saved.
But really?
You're just learning how to drown quieter.
And by the time I realized I wasn't rescued—
just rearranged—
it was too late.
I'd already traded one kind of cage for another.
And loyalty don't buy you freedom.
It just buys you chains with a different shine.

When he went M.I.A. on me alls' a sudden, I could have left well enough alone....

Two weeks of quiet split me open—
Selma on my case, me pretending I didn't hear.
I walked circles around that phone like it could bite.
Maybe he forgot. Maybe he moved on.
Maybe I was only a moment to him.
But loneliness is a loud salesman.

I caved.

25

"Candy Business"

"Girl, just call him! Quit overthinkin' it!"

But I was scared.

I must've picked up that phone a dozen times—

like it was a hot potato that might explode if I actually used it.

Bubba-Ray was trouble.

The kind of trouble with its own theme song and warning label.

And me?

Apparently, I was bored enough to ignore both.

Nervous as a cat in a room full of rocking chairs,

I finally hit dial. Beeeeeep.

"Hey, this is Hubba Bubba. Leave a message and I'll shout at ya later."

Hubba Bubba???

What kinda silly ass name is that, bubblegum mascot?

Relief washed over me like a cold beer—

he didn't answer.

I hung up so fast you'd think I was being chased by the fBI.

Next day, he called me back.

My heart did that stupid little jump,

like a puppy who hasn't learned strangers can be serial killers.

"Hey," he drawled. *"You called?"*

"Yeah," said it all smooth and cool like I hadn't just panic-hung up the day

before.

Meanwhile, inside my head: *Girl... you're a mess.*
His voice brightened.
"Glad you did. Wanna see a movie tonight?"
"I have work."
"Call in sick," he pushed.
I bit my lip.
I was broke.
My hours were crap.

"Okay," I breathed. *"I'll call in."*
"Cool. I'll pick you up around seven."
"What do you even do for work
that you can just leave whenever you want?"
He laughed.
"Run my own construction business.
Don't answer to anyone."
I rolled my eyes, but I smiled anyway.
"Seven it is."
I hung up with a flutter in my chest.
He was a linebacker at Baton Rouge Delta Cats – *"fast. Mean. Slightly drunk."* State University,
bigger, taller—built like a vending machine that sold bad decisions—
and there I was, buyin' 'em up like it was my last meal before rehab.
He was too slick.
Too pretty.
Way outta my league.
But I was lonely.
I paced my little livin' room,
tryin' on every halfway decent outfit I owned.
Woke up Orie with all my stompin' around.
I scooped him up and spun him in my arms.

"Mommy's goin' on a date!" I crooned,
even though I was half sick to my stomach about it.
He squealed and giggled.
But later, Bubba-Ray called back.
Plans changed.
He had *"business"* to take care of—
wanted me to ride along.
I didn't even think twice.
I was flattered he wanted me with him at all.
I called Orion's mama to see if she'd keep lil Orie overnight,
threw on my best clothes,
and bolted when I heard his horn.
On the drive, he talked the whole time.
Money.
Cars.
The good ol' days on the football field.
I sat quiet, half-listenin',
half-wishin' I'd stayed home.
Music was bumpin'—
that early 2000s *"I'm a baller, shot caller"* shit.
We was fist-bumpin' through red lights,
actin' like we were untouchable.
It was them *"Charge It to the Game"* days—
when you ain't have shit,
but the fake swagger made it feel like you did.
Then he pulled up to the four Seasons—right there in the Quarter.
All valet lights, marble columns, and illusion.
I blinked.
"What are we doin' here?"
He sighed, like I was the one actin' shady.
"I get a room if I'm gonna be drinkin'.
Safer. Also where I do my business."
"Your... construction business?" I asked, arms crossed.

He snorted.
"No, sweetheart. My candy business."
I blinked.
"Candy?"
He grinned.
"Coke. I sell to strip club owners.
Don't make that face.
It's just till I get on my feet."
I sat back against the seat.
"Well. This is definitely not what I thought I signed up for tonight."
He gave me the puppy-dog eyes.
"Please? Just stay.
Won't take long.
I like havin' you here."
I should've said no.
But I didn't.
We checked in.
While I sat by the window,
he headed out to *"handle things."*
I watched from behind the curtains—
him flashin' a pistol at some guy in a black Mercedes
before slidin' in.
I didn't even flinch.
Guns.
Drugs.
It was all familiar enough.
I told myself I was fine.
When he came back,
he had a big brown duffel.
He laid it down real careful, like it was full of glass.
"That didn't take long, huh Boo?" he smirked.
"Sure," I muttered.
He unzipped it and pulled out a brick of cocaine

like he was showin' off a new puppy.
"Ever seen this much blow before?"
"No."
"Wanna line?"
I should've said no.
But I was pissed.
Stuck in a hotel while he ran deals.
"Yeah," I said. *"fuck it."*
He chopped it up on a vinyl sheet.
I cringed at the stains.
"Ew. Is that blood?"
He laughed it off.
"Ha! Yeah, had a crazy nosebleed a while back."
I didn't even question it.
We sat there gettin' high
while he packed little baggies like they were Halloween candy.
I didn't even feel scared.
It felt like any other night I'd made a bad decision—
Except with better coke
and a fancier hotel.
Eventually he said,
"Come on. Let's make some deliveries."
We hit the french Quarter.
He made stops at strip clubs,
flashy bars,
private parties in mansions
with marble floors
and fancy-ass fountains.
He handed me a little baggie and winked.
"Here. Have fun. Be careful though."
I went to the bathroom
and did lines while he went off to *"talk business."*
He disappeared into back rooms.

I didn't ask questions.
I wanted to look hot.
To feel powerful.
To matter.
I was wearin' my little black skirt and new heels.
I watched myself in the mirror
and tried to see someone glamorous
instead of someone desperate.
By dawn,
we'd made over fifty grand in cash.
I sat shotgun, countin' stacks
while he drove.
I didn't think about cops.
Or prison.
Or the fact that he'd lied to me about everything.
I just thought:
This is the life I want.
I didn't know yet

What it would really cost me.

26

Bar Brawlers and Shot Callers

As long as I can remember—since Daddy went to the nut house when I was two—I'd been in some kind of program. Somebody somewhere always decided I needed supervision. I wasn't there to talk about feelings; I was there to be studied, sorted, and watched.

By five, I was already sipping alcohol at Maw Sunny's kitchen table like it was normal... street drugs like they were legal, and if anybody was watching, well—whoever "they" were—*I* was the free entertainment and the walking research report. Especially in what I now call the Bubba-Ray era.

Bubba Ray and I were a known set.

Bar brawlers, dangerous, and a little too proud of it.

People would step aside when we walked into a room.

We were chaos clowns with strong drugs and bad reputations.

Every now and then, some hero type would hear Bubba running his mouth at me or shoving me around and think they could save me.

That usually ended with Bubba knocking the guy out cold and me finishing off any woman who tried to jump in.

We'd leave arm in arm, sometimes even in the back of a cop car—but it never stuck.

Then there was the time I thought it'd be funny to take the blue pool-table chalk and draw a perfect little circle around the peephole on our front door.

A little "good morning, idiot" in chalk form.

Terrible idea.

He goes to the bathroom.

And that's when the panic hits.

It was 1999, and I'd already been spooking him for weeks, tellin'um Y2K was gonna flip the world upside down and that he needed to get right with Jesus or at least organize his sock drawer.

I'm pretty sure he took that as *"I better do all the cocaine in St. Faux Parish. before the world ends."*

Cause there he was tweakin' at the peep hole like he was auditionin' for a government paranoia study."

"You hear that?"

"No."

"Shhh, ... hear it now?"

"Uh,...Nope..."

"Oh Lord, this is it... this is how I go..." like he's narrating his own documentary. He's pacing, breathing hard, convinced he's dying.

"I'm turning purple,...I think I'm dead Ramey, why are you laughing?"

But before I could tell him its a joke. *HE GONE!*

Running full speed screaming, "I'm going to confession before my soul leaves my body!"

And I'm standin' there on the porch, watchin' him sprint toward the church.

I finally find him hours later in the confession booth.

Except it was the Danny's Fried Chicken up the street, in a stand off with the cops, locked in the poker-machine room...demanding an exorcism before the Millennium.

If we weren't fighting each other, we were fighting somebody else.

Didn't matter if it was a bar, a backyard, or a gas station at two in the morning—violence followed us like stray dogs sniffin' out scraps.

He'd light up the room with that crooked grin, order a round like he owned the place, and it was all downhill from there.

Somebody always had something to say about his mouth, his boots, or me.

Especially me.

If a man so much as looked at me sideways, Bubba was already squaring up.

And when Bubba swung, I swung too.

Didn't matter if it was against bikers twice our size or some poor fool who just said the wrong word at the wrong time.

We weren't just a couple.

We were a spectacle.

People didn't ask, *"Is there gonna be a fight?"* when we walked in.

They asked, *"How bad is it gonna get?"*

I remember one night at the Blue Lantern.

The band was playin' "Closing Time[20]," lights dimming like a last call warning, when Bubba slammed his beer on the bar and roared, "You talkin' to my girl?"

The man he was pointing at hadn't even looked my way—least I don't think he had—but by then it was too late.

Chairs scraped, glasses shattered, fists flew.

Somebody pulled me by the hair.

Bubba laughed through the chaos, eyes wild, black, and vacant — like somebody had unplugged him and he was still running on fumes. I swung one leg behind the gal who thought she had me, and she went down with the kind of speed that made it look less like self-defense and more like I'd accidentally hit the "demo mode" button on myself.

Then headed for the exit, shit I was on probation.

Then I heard the crash as the entire front window exploded outward.

I froze, one foot in the doorway, watching Bubba's rage go nuclear.

A big fucker went through that front glass like a rag doll.

Bubba grabbed my arm and shouted, *"Awe, fuck, let's get out of here!"*

We left skid marks out the parking lot and never looked back.

Truth was, we were just raw nerves and whiskey, playing out our hurt where the whole world could see.

And I thought that was power.

Thought making people scatter when we walked in meant we mattered.

But power built on fear don't last.

It eats itself.

Looking back, I see it plain:

Those nights weren't about fun or pride.

They were just rehearsals for worse things waiting in the wings.

Blood as a prelude.

Bruises as practice.

Chaos as a warm-up act.

And we were the headliners nobody asked for.

That was my normal—violence on a loop,

always followed by the same pattern: blackout, regret, repeat.

And every time I promised myself I'd do better,

I'd find myself staring down another empty bottle,

wondering if I was born this way or if I'd just stopped caring somewhere along the line, knowing deep in my soul none of it would ever be the magic pill that would fix me.

27

Billy Said Go Bye Bye

It was late afternoon.
I was off work,
spendin' time with Orie in the same yard
where I used to play with Daddy & cousin Buzz.
The grass was overgrown in spots,
the oak tree's branches casting long shadows.
Orie was almost two now,
his wild blonde curls peekin' out from under a tiny cowboy hat.
We were playin' fetch with a rubber ball,
takin' turns rollin' it across the uneven yard.
He squealed with delight each time he chased it down.
I laughed, clappin' my hands.
"Good job, buddy! Bring it back to Mama."
But one throw bounced sideways
and rolled under a thick tangle of brush
at the edge of the yard.
Orie toddled over,
pushing into the green,
outta sight for a second.
"Hey, careful over there," I called, watchin' close.
He didn't answer.

A few seconds later he backed out slowly,
but he didn't have the ball.
Instead, he was clutchin' somethin' in his little fist.
"Baby? Where's the ball?"
Before he could answer,
a pickup truck rattled into the driveway.
I froze.
Bubba-Ray climbed out,
unannounced,
lookin' around like he owned the place.
My stomach dropped.
"Hey," he called, flashin' that devilish grin.
I forced a tight smile.
"Hi. You weren't supposed to come by today."
Bubba-Ray ignored my tone
and sauntered over, crouching in front of Orie.
"Whatcha got there, buddy?" he asked, sing-songy.
Orie stared at him warily,
then slowly opened his palm.
Inside was an old, dirt-caked baby doll eye—
just one milky eye, chipped at the edge, cased in baby doll rubber.
Bubba-Rays' eyes narrowing in on the object.
"The hell is that?"
Orie looked up at him, dead serious.
"Billy said go bye-bye."
A chill ran up my spine.
Bubba-Ray frowned, shiftin' uncomfortable.
"Hey now, that's creepy," he muttered.
I reached for my son.
"Okay, baby, let's go inside."
But Orie squirmed.
Turned back toward Bubba-Ray and yelled:
"Billy said go bye-bye*!*"

His voice was shrill, insistent.
It was the first time he'd ever seen Bubba-Ray,
but I could feel it—
my son knew.
It wasn't like he hadn't seen other men around—
Chalk Line Charlie, Lob, Shawz, and Moose were always over visitin'.
But even at barely two years old,
he sensed something was off.
He stomped over to Bubba-Ray,
hit at his pant leg.
"Go away! Go away!"
Bubba-Ray's smirk dropped. He stood up, jaw tight.
"I'll just go," he snapped.
"Okay," I said, sharper than I meant. "Well… bye."

For half a heartbeat, something small and stupid flickered in me — the tiniest thought that maybe, since he was only the second person I'd ever been with, I should at least *try* to make this work. But the feeling passed as quick as it came.

I shifted Orie on my hip and stepped outside, steadying myself.

"Bubba-Ray," I said, "this ain't workin'. You're bothered by my son, and I'm not livin' like that. We should go our separate ways."

I had wanted to believe this could work.
I adored Orie—he was my whole world.
Half the time I didn't even know where Bubba-Ray was
or what he was doin'.
And when I couldn't come along,
he rubbed it in my face
with all the fun I was missing.
I was so tired of bein' sad.

He turned on me, furious.

"Whatcha said?"

I swallowed hard,
feelin' the words fight their way out.
"Bubba-Ray, I don't think this is workin'.
I can tell you're bothered by my son,
and I can't do that.
We should go our separate ways."
Silence.
Then he spat in my face.
"I was just fuckin' you anyway.
Stupid bitch."
Rage and horror collided in my chest.

Him being the only other person that seen me naked besides Orion,
Oh Hell Naw!
I slapped that big hairy ugly bastard as hard as I could!
Oh Oh abort abort... too late.
In a blink, he lunged.
Grabbed me by the throat.
Slammed me into the front post of the porch.
I kicked.
Clawed.
But he was too strong.

Blackness crept in at the corners of my vision— and in the static of my brain, Eric's old robot voice cut through the fog: *Abort. Abort.*

Then Daddy's voice rose up behind it, soft and apologetic, the way he'd never sound unless he meant it: *Baby... I'd help you if I was still alive.*

And the world cut to black.

He dropped me.

I hit the ground hard, gasping for air, my throat burning like it had been branded. Orie's cries cut through the haze, sharp and desperate, and I wanted to scream back, to tell him I was okay, but the words stuck in my chest like splinters. Bubba-Ray's shadow loomed over me, his voice dripping with venom, and I felt the weight of every bad choice I'd ever made pressing down on me. How did I get here? How did I let this happen? I wanted to believe I was strong, that I could survive anything, but in that moment, I felt small. Smaller than I'd ever been.

I crumpled to the ground, gaspin'.
From inside came my son's terrified cries:
"Mommy! Mommy!"
Bubba-Ray glared down at me.
"I got friends in high places. Don't fuck with me.
Call the cops, and someone close to you will get slaughtered.
Go take care of your boy."
And I believed him.
His mama lived over the Intracoastal in Larouxville.
Daddy always called Larouxville Beverly Hills
because the houses were bigger
and the people acted fancier.
Once, ridin' with Bubba-Ray, I saw it for myself.
He pulled into his neighbor's driveway—
a parish judge everybody knew.
They exchanged envelopes
right there in broad daylight.
The judge patted Bubba-Ray on the shoulder.
"Well, that oughta take care of it.
Be like it never happened."
Then Bubba-Ray turned to me with that smug grin:
"This is your first lesson in politics."
He spat at the ground.
Climbed into his truck.
Roared away.
I scrambled back inside,
shakin' all over.
Locked the door.
Scooped up Orie.
Rocked him.

Whispered:

"It's okay, baby. It's okay. Mama's here."

And as I held my son close, his tiny arms wrapped around my neck, I swore I'd never let him see me like this again. Never let him think this was what love looked like.

The bruises were blooming fast, and all I could think was that I'd carved that vow in bone—I'll bleed before my children bleed. But maybe the vow should've been that they'd never have to see me bleed at all.

I rocked him, whispering soft, even as my throat throbbed under my fingers. And I wondered, What kind of shit did I get myself into now?

28

P.U.S.H.

So I did that dumb shit for a couple of years.
Because, of course—
low and behold—
I was pregnant.
Again.
Mama said she'd help. She meant it, too.
But I had to wonder:
Had I just become a glutton?
for pain? for chaos?
for chasing down broken men
like they came with fixable instructions?

Orion and I had, for a brief moment,
considered getting back together.
He was trying.
Showing up.
fixing things around the house.
Sitting with me on the porch like we used to.
And for the first time in a long time,
I'd let myself wonder *what if*.
Then I found out I was pregnant.

I didn't tell him.
Not at first.
I'd lay awake at night,
staring at the ceiling,
trying to figure out how to say it.
Hey, so... funny story. This baby ain't yours.

I really don't even know how I survived Bubba's crazy-ass.
He destroyed everything we owned.
Not little stuff. Everything.
Cracked the TV screen in a rage.
Tore doors off hinges.
Split the waterbed wide open
during some drug-fueled blackout—
gallons of water soaking everything in its path.
I came home to find my daddy's old pictures—
the few I'd managed to keep safe all these years—
floating in it like trash.
Ruined.
And Mama?
She showed up with a damn ax.
Later, she told me why.
Bubba-Ray's mama had hunted her down at the library,
askin' where we were stayin'.
Said Bubba-Ray had just busted into his daddy's gun case
and told her he was gonna end both of our lives.
And he nearly did.
Mama didn't hesitate.
She showed up with the cops—and that ax.

Said she thought about Daddy that day…
about the time he pulled an ax on her
for nearly killing my ass in 89'.
She never swung it.
But I know she wanted to.
Screaming.
Ready to swing.
Hellfire in her eyes.
He treated me like he hated me.
And somehow…
I still couldn't get rid of him.
He always came back.
I don't understand people like that.
But I understood this:
I was always in trouble,
and he had connections I just didn't have anymore.
I don't understand me back then either.
Today, I can't even imagine
letting someone like that near my child—
or my soul.
But back then?
I thought love meant endurance.
I thought surviving him meant I was strong.
I didn't know surviving *myself* would be the hardest part.
Over time, I started changing too.
I'd fight at the drop of a hat.
Rage and shame sat just beneath my skin,
waiting for any excuse to boil over.
I blacked out a lot back then—
woke up in strange places,
with strange people,
unsure how I got there.
I blamed it on the drugs.

And yeah… that was part of it.
But not all.
Not even close.
Selma was found hung.
They said suicide.
But I knew better.
We all did.
And when I asked too many questions,
we had to move out of Aunt Rue's house.
Just like that—
bagged up our life
and hit the road.
Bubba-Ray got his hands on one of those ice chests
that washed up on the beach—
packed full of cocaine.
People were whispering about it for weeks.
And for a while,
he played kingpin.
But the money and the drugs ran out,
like they always do.
And when they did,
we were living out of garbage bags,
bouncing from one friend's couch to the next
like ghosts.
I'd stare in the mirror and wonder:
How did I let it get like this?

One night, I blacked out so hard
I came to in the ER.

They told me I'd tried to kill myself.
I didn't remember a thing.
Just that cold white ceiling
and the weight of something I couldn't name
sitting on my chest.
At some point after that,
I asked Mama if she loved me.
Just blurted it out—
still halfway stitched together from pain and pills.
She said yes.
I asked, *"Why, Mama? 'Cause it's hard to tell sometimes."*
She said nothin'.
That silence stuck to me like a bruise.

Around that time,
Mama wrote me a letter.
I didn't open it right away.
I didn't feel worthy of it.
But eventually, I did.
And when I read it,
I broke.
Then I started to rebuild—
not fast,
not all at once,
but piece by piece.

Dearest Ramey,

When I froze up today and couldn't spit out one good reason why I love you, it's because there wasn't just one good reason I could come up with...

You're mine to love.

I love you because I'm supposed to.

I don't know WHY I love you — I just do.

You are a part of me, but not me, yet you're all the better parts of me... all that I wasn't.

The things I love about you are your great personality,

your courage,

the wonderful mom you are.

You're a warm, giving, and loving person.

Not only that, you're creative in so many ways.

You know how to dress, how to fix your hair, and you're truly gifted as an artist with your paintings and drawings.

Ramey, you don't even have to try to look nice.

You're naturally beautiful all the time.

This morning on the news, a psychiatrist talked about the mother/daughter relationship and how it's one of the most difficult.

I'm sorry ours has always been so strained.

Unfortunately, I made all my mistakes with you.

Had my spirit not been broken at such an early age,

I would have been a better parent.

At 44, I'm still growing up.

If my mom had been there for me when I was little,

I would have learned how to nurture.

But I never knew and never learned it.

I can encourage, but I don't know how to nurture

(I kill plants and pets — is it any wonder I would hurt my children?).

I don't have to like your friends or the color of your hair,

and we don't have to agree on anything...

I will always love you.

You are my firstborn and the first person who never abandoned me, even when I had those emotional walls up.

Things have changed.

We are both women now, raising our children together.

We finally made it, don't you think?

I'm really sorry you're so tired

and need a break from the kids and I'm not there for you.

Before I forget...

if you're still trying to "win my approval"

or worried about living up to my expectations — let it go.

I have never lived up to yours.

for whatever reason, I was never the mom you may have wanted,

but I'm the only one you've got — defective.

Be your own person, Ramey, flaws and all.

Stop losing sleep over everyone else;

let them lose sleep over you for a change.

All I ever wanted for you was the best of everything.

The best education, the best job in something you truly love, the best husband.

I never wanted you mistreated or in relationships that weren't good for you.

That really angered me.

Like any parent, I wanted to protect you — and still do.

I'll try to stay out of your business,

but it's hard when I know better and can help you make better choices.

My hardheaded girl — you always were stubborn.

No matter what choices you make for yourself,

I will always be there for you

(whether I like your choices or not).

Getting better is a lifelong process.

You will win your battles — and you will have many.

You're my favorite person.

Remember to P.U.S.H.

Pray Until Something Happens.

The road to success is always under construction.

I will always love you...

Mom

P.S. Forgive yourself. God, Jesus, and all of us already have.

I was still slowly unraveling.
Everywhere we went,
we carried crazy with us—
like a stain that wouldn't wash out.
And no matter how bad things got,
he still found ways to make me feel
like I was the problem.
But there was one thing I knew wasn't the problem.
My son.
Orie was the only light I had left.
And if anybody—*anybody*—
thought they could put their hands on him…
They were about to learn what kind of girl I really was.

29

The Inheritance?

Little Orie could play for hours without another soul around. Didn't matter if the yard was bare or the TV cut off—he'd still conjure whole worlds out of thin air. Power Rangers lined up like soldiers, Hot Wheels wrecking into villains nobody else could see. Even that old G.I. Joe missing an arm became a hero when Orie held him.

He didn't just play. He gave them voices. Made them argue, plead, beg for their lives, then clap like thunder when the right one won.

When the cable got shut off after his daddy left, I thought maybe Orie would come undone. But he just ran our *Toy Story* tape ragged. Wore it down until the VCR whined in protest. He knew every word by heart.

"Buzz Lightyear never gives up," he told me one night, dead serious, like that line alone could keep the walls from caving in.

Then came Billy.

It was just a plastic doll eye, cracked and scratched, half-buried in the dirt. Nothing attached. No face, no body, just the eye. But Orie found it like treasure. Held it in his fist and said, "This is Billy."

From that day on, everything ran through Billy. The Power Rangers weren't just his anymore—they were Billy's team. The cars were Billy's cars. Even bedtime was Billy's call.

"Billy says go to sleep now, Mama."

I didn't think it was cute. Not really. It gnawed at me, the way Eric used to. That damned skull, staring at me with those glassy blue doll eyes. I used to wonder why I never questioned it, why I never thought to just put it away.

And now here was Orie, clutching Billy everywhere he went, like it had always been waiting for him. Like I'd missed it somehow, just the way I once missed what Eric really was.

That's what rattled me most—the familiarity.

Because Eric didn't just appear. He was passed. Handed down to my daddy with a story I still don't understand.

And what if Billy wasn't just some cracked toy Orie stumbled across? What if Billy was passed too? What if the things we carry don't belong to us at all, but move through us like shadows in the bloodline—watching, waiting, choosing?

I didn't tell Orie that. I just let him hold Billy, whisper for Billy, obey Billy. And I prayed he'd let it go before it sank its hooks in, the way Eric once sank into me.

Billy ran the show.

It didn't matter what we were doing—eating, shopping, driving down the bayou—Billy had the final word.

"Billy says buckle your seatbelt, Mama," Orie would warn me, serious as a deacon. And if I didn't click it fast enough? He'd gasp like I'd just sinned.

"Billy says you gon' fly through the windshield if you don't listen."

Even snack time became a theological debate. "Billy says no green Skittles—they poison."

Instead of tossing them out, Orie started saving them in a Mason jar under his bed. Weeks later, the Skittles had melted into one giant, neon-green brick. He held it up like the Ten Commandments and declared, "Billy says this is the Emerald Tablet."

By then, even strangers were in on it. At the Piggly Wiggly, Orie staged a whole standoff in aisle three because "Billy says the cart don't want that brand of toilet paper." I'm standing there with a 12-pack in my hands, red-faced, while my six-year-old yells, "Mama, Billy said DOUBLE-PLY ONLY!" like we were about to get audited by the Lord himself behind it.

The cashier didn't even blink. She slid our groceries across the scanner, leaned in, and whispered, "Billy approves," before handing me the receipt like it was a secret covenant.

The absurdity peaked one night when Orie marched into the living room wearing Maw Maw's old Mardi Gras beads, the doll eye tied to the end like a necklace. He climbed up on the coffee table, spread his arms wide, and shouted,

"Billy says I'm the king now!"

Then he made us all clap while he tapped the dog on the head with a fly swatter. Poor Boudreaux just sat there, tail wagging, officially crowned *Sir Bark-a-Lot, Protector of the House.*

Daddy would've laughed himself sick, but I couldn't. Because as wild and ridiculous as it was—the Skittle bricks, the toilet paper trials, the coronation of the damn dog—it all had that same weight I remembered from Eric. That eerie way a joke stopped being a joke once you realized it might've come from somewhere else.

It started creeping into places Billy had no business being.

At church, Orie refused to bow his head unless Billy said so. Pastor asked us to pray, and my boy sat there stiff as a board, one eye squinting at the doll eye in his pocket like he was waiting for clearance. When he finally whispered, "Billy says okay," the whole congregation heard it, and half the pews cracked up. The other half looked like they'd seen blasphemy crawl straight out of the hymn book.

At Mama's Sunday table, it turned into full-on theater. Orie sat at the kids' end, solemn as a judge, repeating Billy's decrees:

"Billy says no one gets cornbread till the beans are blessed." "Billy says Uncle Noose can't have sweet tea 'cause he lies too much." "Billy says Maw Maw's gumbo's too salty this week."

The whole table froze, forks mid-air. Maw Maw's ladle clattered against the pot like a gavel. Eustis almost choked on his rice, sputtering, "Now who the hell is Billy?"

And me? I just stared at my boy, his small fingers curled around that cracked plastic eye like it was a relic passed down from the Vatican itself.

The worst was Christmas Eve.

All the cousins gathered, wrapping paper flying, everybody wild. Orie stood in the middle of the living room, holding Billy up like the Ark of the Covenant. His little voice rang out over the noise:

"Billy says—only the pure of heart get presents."

Every adult in the room laughed like it was the cutest thing they'd ever heard, but my stomach turned clean over. Because it didn't feel like play anymore.

What child says shit like that?

He used words he didn't pick up from the fools I kept company with, and his daddy had the I.Q. of a roach turd.

It felt like doctrine written in a stranger's hand. Not divine. Not innocent.

More like the hand that rocks the cradle— and rewrites the lullaby while you sleep.

30

Welcome to the New Regime

Bubba-Ray wrote me letters from the mental ward.
I left them unopened on the counter next to the Entergy bill.
I wasn't interested in another loop around that ride.
Orion started coming around again—
but this time he brought something new:
Medea.
She was pretty in that *I make lists about people I hate* kind of way.
Manicured, measured, and full of quiet judgment.
And she didn't want Orion anywhere near me.
Didn't even want him picking up Orie from my house.
So she started doing it herself.
I didn't like it.
Neither did my son.
One afternoon, she pulled up early in her car,
honked like she was ordering fast food,
and stomped up the steps like she paid rent.
"Let's go, little man," she chirped, reaching for him.
He backed up, hid behind me.
"Noooo!" he wailed. *"I don't want to go!"*
She grabbed Orie by the arm—
snatched him up like I wasn't even standing there.

He started crying.
"No! I want Mama!"
Tears rollin', feet draggin'.
And I just stood there.
Dumbfounded.
For a second, I didn't move.
I watched it play out like I was outside my own body.
And in that stillness, I thought about it—
how she looked at me like I was nothing.
How she reached for my son like I was a stray dog and he was her prize.
How she turned her back to walk off, like I'd already lost.
And I'll be damned if I was about to let this gal
make me look like a cur in front of my baby.
Because this right here?
This wasn't Mama's blood, baby. **This was mine.**
So I broke her nose.
Sharp. Loud. final.
My hand burned.
My pride didn't.
And in that one breath of silence right after the crack?
I could just hear Daddy in the clouds somewhere,
laughin' through a puff of Kool cigarette smoke:
"Ohhh Slick... you in trouble now."
Her eyes went wide.
She stumbled back, cuppin' her face.
Back in Mama and Daddy's time,
you took your lick and you went on home.
Handled it in the yard.
Called it even.
But this?
This was a different world.
She called the cops
before the blood even stopped runnin'.

And Sheriff Lukeroy wasn't runnin' shit no more.

'89 took his eye, his badge, his throne. Shot down and shuffled off. He'd crawl back years later — not as king of the parish, but as a paper man. Probation officer. The system's lapdog.

The old crew was gone. Buck in the ground. Grom's boys scattered, dead, or silent.

This was the new regime.

And it wasn't his.

They were gone.

The ones who'd slide you a warning before a warrant—

No more heads-up calls.

No more backdoor mercy.

Just cold paperwork and a name they already decided guilt for.

Now?

I was just another angry girl with a record.

No allies.

No favors.

No second chances.

I was on the wrong side of the law

and the wrong side of law enforcement.

I had pushed just about any and er'body out of my life, thinking if I kept 'em out of the friction, they wouldn't get burned. All I really did was make sure nobody was close enough to catch me when I fell.

And worst of all?

Somewhere between that punch and that cell, between Daddy's laugh and Medea's blood, it hit me:

I didn't have a single man left who'd ride for me… but heaven help the fool who forgets I ain't ridin' alone. Amen.

31

Midnight Mercy

Besides the new charge, I already had a DWI[21] on my record. Walked straight into a neighbor's house one night, high as a kite, and took their truck like it was mine. Wrecked it right into Bayou Glass—a locally owned shop.

Fittin', right? Shattered glass, shattered girl.

Maw Sunny—now a millionaire livin' off interest—paid the restitution. No questions, no lecture. Just did it.

But that didn't mean I wasn't in the fight of my life. Because that's when he showed up.

Ronin Lukeroy. Sheriff turned probation officer. Cowboy hat pulled low, suit jacket over blue jeans, boots scuffed, black eye patch cuttin' his face in half like judgment itself.

Truth is, it wasn't my first brush with him. One night on Atomic Lane, the cops raided the trap house I was in. Didn't find a damn thing, but they cuffed us anyway and stuck me in the back of a patrol car, headlights cutting through the dawn haze.

Lukeroy stood across the street by a cruiser, talkin' low to a deputy, eyes on paperwork—

I'd only seen the sheriff a handful of times when I was little, doorways, cookouts, those grown-folk rooms kids weren't supposed to hover in—the hat and patch were enough to brand anybody's memory.

Then came Saint Mama, bless her heart. Marchin' up the street in her long baby-blue nightgown with big fluffy clouds all ore' it, swingin' a log with a nine-inch nail hammered through the top.

I remember thinkin', Oh Lord Mama, I'm too high for this shit.

High are not she was comin' through the morning fog like she was floatin' down from heaven itself— looked like she'd plucked a telephone pole to crucify me on.

Symbolic now that I think about it. My life's always been animated like that—equal parts tragic and cartoon.

She wasn't comin' to negotiate; she was comin' to haul me home.

Lukeroy said somethin' short to the uniforms, calm as a tide change, and the scene cooled like a pot pulled off the burner.

I recognized him from back then, sure. Didn't mean he'd place me now.

I'm the one who remembers everybody—names, faces, the way a foot drags after a long day. I'm sure I looked different—hair, weight, weather, the fact I hadn't slept for 2 years— but once I learn your name, it welds in. I can spot your face under thirty years of sin and rot.

The funny part is, don't matter if I'm deep in mess, people still wanted to be around me. Maybe they saw somethin' I didn't.

Folks'd corner me in the grocery line, spillin' their hearts like they were sittin' in my chair back at the old house. Didn't matter if I was clean or twisted— they'd talk, and I'd listen.

Guess that's what happens when your hands were made to fix things. Sometimes prayer don't sound holy— it sounds like gossip said gentle.

And sometimes God hides His work in women like I was back then— tired, broke, all washed up at 22.

I was sittin' in that probation lobby, fillin' out intake forms.

Big brotha next to me—tattoos up his neck, leaned over like we were old friends in the same sinking boat.

"Who they assign you to?" he asked, voice low, like he already knew it'd be bad.

I didn't even look up. "Lukeroy."

He froze. "Damn… girl. What you did?"

I shrugged, because hell if I knew which charge finally tipped the scales.

He shook his head slow, like he was watchin' a car wreck in real time. "Nah, you don't get it. Lukeroy don't *take* people. Man picks one case every decade, maybe. And if he picked you?" He leaned back, whistled through his teeth. "Shit. Good luck. Word is he loves his job a little too much. He'll be sittin' in the yard when you walk out that door."

My stomach dropped clean through the floor. I'd been arrested, raided, cuffed, detoxed, dragged, dumped, and resurrected—but that right there? That rattled me.

Because if Lukeroy wanted you… he already had a plan.

* * *

Pen tappin', voice flat. "Some do half your dirt and vanish into a cell. You land in treatment again. Hmm. Curious."

He let it hang. "Why you think you're so lucky, Knuckles?"

That name hit like déjà vu—tasted old, like salt in a split lip. Brought back the saltwater dreams that stalked me before Daddy died.

And no, I ain't got nobody pullin' strings for me and I sure as hell ain't no rat-snitch.

"Maybe I'm blessed," I said, though it came out more like a question.

He didn't smile. Just stared long enough for my skin to itch. "Maybe," he said. "Or maybe the same people that made you lucky are still watchin' to see what you do with it."

I didn't know what the hell that meant then. But I do now.

* * *

Orion had married Medea on a whim, and you could see the regret sittin' in his eyes like bad whiskey.

It hurt him, what they were doin' to me. Maybe he was in over his head too. Or maybe he was just tired.

Either way, it didn't matter. The custody battle had started.

I thought about Mama a lot durin' that time— how she'd found God and changed her life. How she fought all the way to the Supreme Court for my baby sister— the first deaf child in St. faux Parish to get an interpreter.

They wanted to ship her off to Baton Rouge School for the Deaf like she was a lost cause. But Mama wasn't havin' it.

"She's not retarded," she said. "She is perfectly capable. Her only issue is that she cannot hear. I will not send her away over that."

And she didn't. Because she won.

That spirit—that fire—it lived in me too, even if it was buried under mess.

Now, my beliefs ain't what they were back then, but I know what prayer with intent mixed with a little action behind it can do.

Back then, I truly believed it was the rosary— prayin' to Mary—that turned the tide.

Because after months of court drama, after feelin' like I was screamin' into a system that didn't hear women like me...

Midnight. There was a knock at the door.

And lo and behold, it was The Orions—both of 'em— standin' there with every single one of his belongings in tow.

He'd tried to leave Medea. Tried to escape. Her family blocked the driveway. So he just drove through them.

Scratched the hell outta that pearl-white SUV. Didn't care.

He brought my son back to me. And I knew then—I'd already won.

Next morning in court, I walked in with my child in my arms. Big Orion sat alone. And to my surprise, his whole family—the ones who'd watched me fail—came to sit behind me.

Mama saw it before I did. Saw the way his people shook their heads at him, disgust written plain as daylight. Saw how he shrank under it, shoulders caving like a man already halfway buried.

I watched Mama's eyes meet his—steady, soft, unflinching. And without a word, she stood up, walked across that courtroom, and sat beside him.

She didn't do it for show. She did it because she knew what it felt like to be the one everybody gave up on.

He was already defeated. But Mama wasn't there to twist the knife. She was there to remind me:

It's okay to be humble in victory. 'Cause ain't nobody wins when the family is broke.

And in that moment—my son on my hip, Mama bridging the divide, his family sitting behind *me*— I realized the truth:

I hadn't just won a custody battle. I'd survived a war that tried to take everything from me. And somehow, through all the mess and madness, the people who were supposed to hate me... chose to stand with me instead.

Maybe they knew something I didn't. Or maybe they just recognized the fire in me Mama had passed down.

Either way, that was the day everything shifted.

32

Scissors and Second Chances

I always said I'd been doing hair since I was old enough to hold a rat-tail comb.

By ten years old I was perming the whole damn neighborhood.

Mama would come home to the kitchen smelling like rotten eggs from those old-school perm kits.

She'd holler, "Ramey, open a window before you gas us all!"

But the mamas kept bringing their daughters over.

"You got a gift," they'd say.

But shit, I knew it wasn't about hair.

People just loved spending time with me.

Maybe it was 'cause I never looked at 'em like they were broken.

I'd laugh with 'em, cry with 'em, and never once tell 'em to hush.

Folks can smell judgment the way dogs smell fear—and I never had none to give.

The chair was my altar long before I ever knew what I was prayin' for.

I'd wash their hair, let the water run warm down their necks, and they'd start talkin'—

about the husbands that left, the pills they hid, the dreams they buried out back with the dogs.

I didn't just listen—I'd yap 'um up right back,

and nine outta ten I'd end up prayin' over 'em or with 'em 'bout somethin'.

Not the kind of prayer you plan,
but the kind that crawls up out your chest and don't take no for an answer.
Next thing you know, they'd have me helpin' clean out their attics,
haulin' boxes, runnin' 'em to the doctor, feedin' cats they swore weren't theirs.
I could hardly say no.
Figured my karma could use somethin' to counteract all the wrong.
And truth be told, helpin' them always felt like helpin' me too—
like God was keepin' score, and for once, I wasn't losin'.
Wasn't the first time I'd seen prayer do its thing,
but it ain't like I ever meant to make it happen.
Sometimes it just came through me,
like a draft blowin' through a screen door nobody fixed.
And no—God didn't answer every little prayer I sent up.
Sometimes He said no.
Sometimes He said not yet.
But every now and then, He'd say just enough to keep me believin'.
So when Miss Eula Mae came in talkin' 'bout her boy locked up two years—
wrong crowd, wrong side of the law—
I already knew what to do.
We bowed our heads while her color set, me holdin' a comb like a cross,
and I asked God to bring that boy home clean.
A week later she come barrelin' in, hollerin' he'd been released—
charges dropped, fingerprints didn't match.
Swore the Lord used my rinse water as holy.
Then came Bobby Jo, the one with lupus and a laugh that rattled glass jars.
Her hair was fallin' out in handfuls.
She told me she'd stopped lookin' in mirrors.
We prayed anyway.
Two months later she came back, hair thick as moss, cheeks pink again.
Said her doctor called it remission.
I called it mercy.
And old man Léo, nearly blind from cataracts,

just wanted a trim so his wife "could see him decent in heaven."
He sat quiet while I worked, then asked if we could pray for peace.
I took his hands, and we did.
When he opened his eyes, tears rolled down both cheeks.
Said he could see the light over my shoulder—said it was her, smilin'.
He died that night in his chair at home, TV still hummin'.
After that, I stopped questionin' it.
The shop weren't just a salon anymore.
It was a halfway house for broken spirits—
a place where the prayers smelled like perm solution
and miracles left streaks of bleach on your apron.
Really, I was busy not dying—pills, potions, and prayers—
and I missed the handwriting on the wall.
It's the whole reason I resurrected this story from the dead.
I nearly forgot it in the haze of drugs, bad choices, and too many nights crying into a bottle—
until I decided I was done bein' the tragedy in my own story.
By golly, I'd be lyin' if I said I did it all on my own.
Truth is, I was in a nice little program straight out the nuthouse—
they called it recovery, I called it purgatory with vending machines.
They handed out meds like communion wafers,
and every swallow felt like signin' a deal I didn't read close enough, and I knew it.

Daddy used to talk about this kinda thing,
Said pharmakeia ran the show—
that the real devils wore lab coats and smiled for cameras.
I didn't wanna believe him;
Did I even knew what made me tick?
Somewhere in the quiet—
between the fluorescent hum of the ward and the rattle of my pill cup—
somethin' started pullin' it out of me,
like the medicine itself had a spirit,

and it wanted a body to live in.
Dr. Reidman said I couldn't quit, not dare to try it.
Said I'd spin off the rails again.
But what if the rails were never mine?
What if they'd been laid there to keep me circlin' the same damned track?
Big Pharma don't cure—
it conditions.
It don't heal—
it harvests.
So I started taperin' off quiet,
just me and the Lord and the ghosts that guard the medicine cabinet.
Every day I felt more like myself—
and more like I was bein' watched.
That's when Sheriff Ronin Lukeroy stopped by the shop,
leanin' in the doorway like a man with bad news he didn't wanna give.
He said he'd been out near Haunt-Bourne,
checkin' into some parish files that didn't line up—
old experiments, new power bills, doors still locked from the inside.
He warned me to stay clear of that place.
Said the kind of science they practiced don't stay in test tubes.
Then he tore a sheet from his notepad, scribbled a name, and slid it over the counter.
"Someone out past Belle Mire," he said,
"a healer who knows what Haunt-Bourne did to people's heads.
Not one of them.
One who got out."
Then he hesitated, thumb hooked in his belt.
"Funny thing, though—the program you were in?
Haunt-Bourne shut it down years ago. Government pulled the plug, locked the records."
I blinked at him.
"Well, that's strange," I said, tryin' to laugh though my mouth went dry.
"'Cause I still meet with them once a month."

Ronin's jaw worked like he wanted to say more,
but all he managed was, "Then somebody's still runnin' the lights."
He tipped his hat and left me there with the paper burnin' a hole in my palm.
That's when I knew this story wasn't done.
It was shapeshiftin', whisperin' through static,
waitin' on somebody brave—or foolish—enough to listen.
And if I didn't write it down,
it was gonna rewrite me instead.
'Cause that's the thing about the past—
just 'cause you buried it don't mean it's dead.
And just because you don't understand somethin'
don't mean it isn't there.

Beauty school was easy.

Gettin' there and back was hell.

I had already started once and dropped out before bitin' the bullet and givin' it another shot.

Had kids to feed, bills screamin' louder than the alarm clock.

Bartended at night, came home to cook supper,

then studied at the sticky kitchen table while the kids fell asleep in front the TV.

There were nights I punched the floor

and screamed into a towel so I wouldn't wake them.

But I didn't quit.

When I passed my state board exam,

I walked out cryin' so hard I couldn't see.

Hugged Emma so tight she squeaked.

"Mommy did it," I whispered.

The old building on the bayou highway was fallin' apart,
but I didn't see the rot—I saw promise.
Rent was cheap 'cause it stank of mildew.
Orion lent me a truck for haulin' supplies—
had to start the damn thing with a screwdriver,
but I appreciated it anyway.
Mama loaned me money for the deposit.
Chalk Line Charlie and Lob helped rip out the carpet,
cussin' and laughin' the whole time.
We painted the walls institution green, and pink—colors I can't escape.
I named it *HeadCases Salon.*
"Crazy people like to get their hair did too—and smoke cigarettes at the same time,"
I told Shawz, who nearly choked on his pop laughin'.
He carved the sign outta driftwood.
I opened *HeadCases* while livin' in a two-story barn.
Not kiddin'.
It had rafters, spiders,
and more haunted energy than a horror movie trailer.
But it was mine, for a spell.
And so was Graton, my potbelly pig,
the shop's unofficial mascot.
Nothin' says *come get your roots touched up*
like a pig named after fried pork.
You really can't make this shit up.
HeadCases: fried-pork mascot,
dollar-store gator mirrors,
one busted shampoo bowl.
I bought a fresh black smock,
dabbed on lipstick I forgot I even owned.
Opening day, I swept the floor twice before anyone showed up.
Emma passed out lollipops.
Orie tried folding towels

but ended up rollin' on the floor with our piggy wiggy.
My first client was old Mrs. Roseau.
"Lord, it's about time someone opened a shop down here," she said,
pressin' triple the payment into my hand.
I bit my lip not to ugly-cry right there.
When the register dinged that first twenty,
I held it up like a trophy.
That night I locked the door, pressed my back to the glass,
and let the tears fall.
I did it, I thought. *I really did.*
I drove home along the bayou, windows down,
warm wind in my face.
Tucked the kids in bed,
sat on the porch in the dark,
listened to the frogs sing.
Whispered a prayer:
"Thank you, Father, for what You've given me and what You've taken away.
For the mercy of another day to try again.
To make it right."

'Cause when trauma's your inheritance,
you better be real careful how you spend it.
But now that I'm writing this all down,
I can't help but notice the patterns.
Just about everyone I started out with is gone.
Mama's gone.
Maw Sunny checked out right after her.
Even Orion didn't make it for the long haul.
Maw Sunny's daddy? Dead at 33.

My mamma's daddy? Dead at 33.

My daddy? Dead at 33.

My son's daddy? … You guessed it, dead at 33!

We didn't kill them.

But sometimes you can't help wondering about curses you don't understand.

But what if it's too late?

33

What We Leave Behind

One night, after closing, I sat on the porch and rolled Eric's old babydoll eye between my fingers.

I stumbled on it during the move into the barn—had near forgot about it.

Lil Orie's Billy talk had done spooked me enough that the first chance I got, I hid the damned thing from him.

Couldn't bring myself to throw it away, though; it was all I had left of Daddy.

When Orie had dug it up one day in the yard,

I wiped it off and didn't think much of it.

But under the porch light, I noticed something I never had before:

a tiny crack across the back, melted together like someone had tried to fix it.

I turned it over.

Pressed my thumb along the seam.

And felt something shift—along with a faint whiff rising up,

rotten-egg and chemical, the same stink that haunted Mama's kitchen on perm days.

Only I hadn't done one of those in years.

It wasn't perm solution.

It was sulfur.

Every hair on my body now standin' at attention.

Inside—barely visible—was a tiny cassette tape.

It would take an act of God—and a lot of asking around—to find the right equipment to hear what was on it.

But that's the thing about the past:
just because you buried it doesn't mean it's dead.
And just because you don't understand it yet
doesn't mean it isn't there.

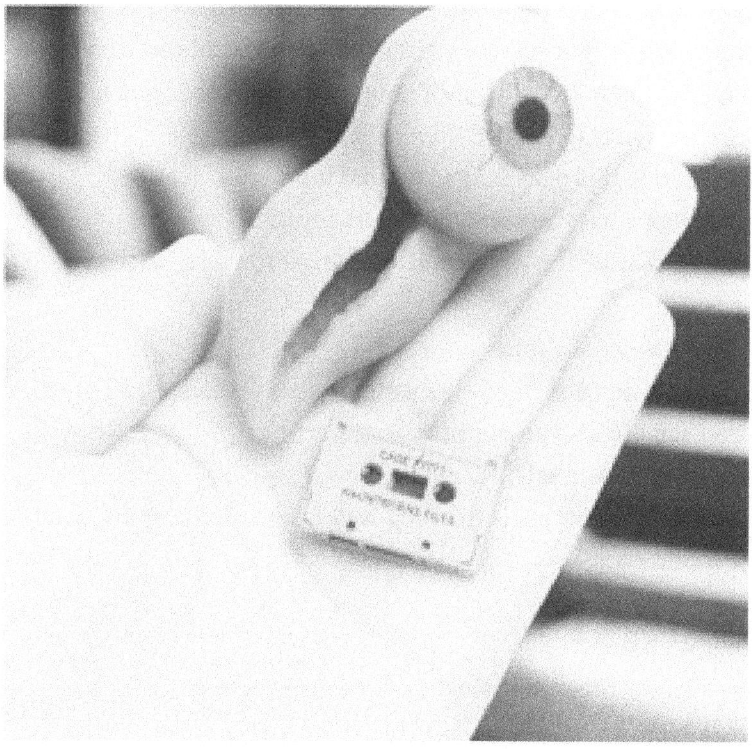

[Tape crackles. Breath hitching. Restrained sobbing.]

October 30th, 1991.

This is Levi.

Sniffling.

"Ramey… baby girl… if you find this… I'm so sorry. God, I can't believe I gotta do this."

Panting.

"Ramey… panting… Ramey… please… listen to me."

Choked sob.

"I—I killed Eric. He's gone."

Breaks into wail.

"But something darker took his place."

[Tape crackles. Breath hitching. Barely restrained sobbing.]

"I'm looking at your picture right now. I don't want you to remember me like this. But I have to tell you—it got me. It's been watching us. Testing us."

"We're not normal, Ramey. Were an experiment."

"I had to hide this tape. Hope you find it before it does."

"Don't trust what you see. Don't trust any of it."

"If you're hearing this, it means it didn't get to this tape."

"Be careful."

Whispers, voice shaking.

"He says his name is Billy. He's watching me—watching all of us. Always. I can't—I can't fight it anymore."

Deep, trembling inhale.

"I'm sorry. This… this is the only way I can stop it. I pray you find this before it finds you."

Cries openly.

it ends with me!

Long silence. Breathing steadies. Low growl rising.

"FUUUUUCKKK YOUUUU BILLLLLYYYY!"

[Tape clicks off.]

…but sadly and systematically it had not ended with daddy, and I was about to be awakened to that revelation in the worst ways humanly possible.

Three generations to break it.

Four to bury it.

And I wasn't about to hand them the shovel.

Eric. Billy. **Knuckles**.

Hmmm, most certainly not the Father, the Son, and the Holy Spirit

Lord have mercy,.... The Unholy trinity,...Maybe *they were* the same haunt. Maybe the same hell-thing.

And now that I remember, I can't shake the thought

... maybe I was never supposed to.

Luke 8:17

> "For nothing is hidden that will not be disclosed, nor anything secret that will not become known and come to light."

Mark 4:22

> "For there is nothing hidden except to be disclosed; nor is anything secret except to come to light."

Closing Note

The line between memory and madness is thinner than swamp mist.

If you think this story's over, you haven't been listening close enough.

Tobacco-Stained Prayers don't end—

they linger, like the last drag on a cigarette you knew better than to light.

THE BAYOU IS OUT OF TIME

Book Two bout'a hit the ground runnin' like the Four Horsemen stole Slick's

cigarettes.

It starts the night The Indian Outlaw—Lil Orie's daddy, local legend,

bare-knuckle cage fighter—

drowns in the St. Faux Bayou.

One minute he's a folk hero.

Next minute he's a ghost.

And that's when the first seal cracks.

Luckroy sends her to meet the only person who ever broke out of

Hauntbourne's mind-trap, and the second their story hits her ears, the whole

world slowly begins to tilt.

Memories snap awake.

Time gets slippery.

The old painting on her wall starts acting like it's been waiting on her.

Something ancient awakening in St. Faux Parish—

and it isn't from this dimension.

Orie's stigmata after the UFO sighting is the first trumpet.

Billy's resurrection-style return is the second.

His near-hanging at twenty-seven—

that's the prophecy roaring to life.
The curse isn't repeating.
It's accelerating.
The ages, the dates, the bloodlines—
it's all been pre-written in Ramey's art, Daddy's warnings,
and a forgotten work published long before she understood its meaning.
Now the bayou is shifting.
Time is folding.
And every unanswered question from Book One becomes a loaded weapon pointed straight at her family.
If Ramey and Luckroy don't rewrite the pattern before Orie turns 33,
It'll have taken "another son" — hers. And she ain't having it. She'll march barefoot on oyster shells, with her toenails unpolished in public before she lets the bayou take her boy the way it took the men before him.
This is where the truth hits like thunder.
Where the veil doesn't just rip—
it burns.
This is where Ramey stops being the cursed...
and becomes the weapon.
The end might be coming...
But so is Ramey.
BOOK TWO: SALTWATER KNUCKLES

Notes

THE END JUSTIFIES THE MEANS

1 **Freddy Krueger** (/□kru□□□r/) is a fictional character and the antagonist of the *A Nightmare on Elm Street* horror film franchise. Created by Wes Craven, he made his debut in Craven's *A Nightmare on Elm Street* (1984) as the malevolent spirit of a child killer who had been burned to death by his victims' parents after evading prison

2 "***Cindi Lauper***"**Cynthia Ann Stephanie Lauper** born June 22, 1953) is an American singer, songwriter and actress.[3] Known for her distinctive image, featuring a variety of hair colors and eccentric clothing,[4] and for her powerful four-octave vocal range,[5] Lauper has sold over 50 million records worldwide.[6

3 **George Alan O'Dowd** (born 14 June 1961), known professionally as **Boy George**, is an English musician, songwriter and DJ who rose to fame as the lead singer of the pop band Culture Club.

4 ***Gremlins*** is a 1984 American black comedy horror film directed by Joe Dante, written by Chris Columbus and starring Zach Galligan, Phoebe Cates, Hoyt Axton, Polly Holliday and Frances Lee McCain, with Howie Mandel providing the voice of Gizmo the *Mogwai*. It draws on legends of folkloric mischievous creatures that cause malfunctions—" gremlins"—in the British Royal Air Force going back to World War II. The story follows Billy Peltzer, who receives Gizmo as a pet, who then spawns more of his kind that evolve into the titular imp-like monsters that wreak havoc on Billy's hometown during Christmas Eve.[2]

INSTITUTION GREEN

5 Being "**locked up in Mandeville**" or " The Nuthouse" meant staying on secure psychiatric wards under 24-hour supervision. Patients with acute symptoms were often kept on locked units for safety, especially if they had a history of **violent episodes or hallucinations** that made them a danger to themselves or othersIn the late 1970s and early 1980s, state hospitals like SELH relied heavily on antipsychotics such as Thorazine and Haldol. High doses often caused heavy sedation and a stiff, shuffling gait commonly known as the "Thorazine shuffle," a well-documented side effect in psychiatric institutions of that era (see *Chlorpromazine*, Wikipedia).

6 **Adrenochrome** is a chemical compound produced by the oxidation of adrenaline (epinephrine). It was the subject of limited research from the 1950s through to the 1970s as

a potential cause of schizophrenia. While adrenochrome has no currently proven medical application, the semicarbazide derivative, carbazochrome, is a hemostatic medication. Adrenochrome is mass produced and commercially available to the public, and is not a controlled substance.[2][3]The treatment of schizophrenia with such potent anti-oxidants is controversial. In 1973, the American Psychiatric Association reported methodological flaws in Hoffer's work on niacin as a schizophrenia treatment and referred to follow-up studies that did not confirm any benefits of the treatment.[12] Multiple additional studies in the United States,[13] Canada,[14] and Australia[15] similarly failed to find benefits of megavitamin therapy to treat schizophrenia.

7 **brisé** *(bree-ZAY)* — casual French expression meaning **a rough head-rub**, usually done in a teasing or affectionate way. Literally "head-rub," but culturally it matches the vibe of **messing up someone's hair with your knuckles in passing**.

8 In Cajun-French, "matou" means "tomcat." Daddy once joked that Mama had a "large cat head," a comment that was more mischief than meaning. It became a running family joke — the kind you laugh at even while insisting it's absolutely not nice.

HIGH HEELS AND HAYMAKERS

9 **Tina Turner** (born **Anna Mae Bullock**; November 26, 1939 – May 24, 2023) was a singer, songwriter, actress, and author. Dubbed the "Queen of Rock 'n' Roll", Turner's vocal prowess, dynamic voice and electrifying stage presence helped to break racial and gender barriers in rock music. She is one of the best-selling music artists of all time, with estimated sales of over 100 million records worldwide.

10 **Robert "Rocky" Balboa** (also known by his ring name the **Italian Stallion**) is a fictional character and the titular protagonist of the *Rocky* franchise. The character was created by Sylvester Stallone, who has also portrayed him in eight of the nine films in the franchise. He is depicted as a working class or poor Italian-American from the slums of Philadelphia who started out as a club fighter and "enforcer" for a local Philly Mafia loan shark. He is portrayed as overcoming the obstacles that had occurred in his life and in his career as a professional boxer.

11 "**Eye of the Tiger**" is a song by the American rock band Survivor. It was written by Frankie Sullivan and Jim Peterik as the theme song for the 1982 film *Rocky III* and released that May as a single from Survivor's third album, *Eye of the Tiger*. The song combines hard rock[3] with a post-disco beat.[4]

12 1. The French term *guêpe* translates to "wasp" in English, referring to various hymenopteran insects of the suborder Apocrita. These insects play ecological roles as predators, limiting populations of mosquitoes and other crop-damaging species. See "Guêpe," Wikipédia, https://fr.wikipedia.org/wiki/Guêpe (accessed November 24, 2025).

E.R.I.C., THE WATCHER

13 **Project MK O.F.T.E.N.** was a covert U.S. Department of Defense program developed in

conjunction with the Central Intelligence Agency (CIA) sometime in the late 1960s. A partner or descendant program of MKULTRA, the goal of MKOFTEN was to "test the behavioral and toxicological effects of certain drugs on animals and humans".[1] Testing of these drugs was done on animals, prisoners at Holmesburg Prison in Philadelphia, and military personnel at Edgewood Arsenal.[1]

THE COST TO KILL A BADGE

14 Hühner: German word for chicken

BIG BROTHERS' WATCHING

15 Chobley: loosley based off of Chopsley from Margus the Magificant

THE MISFIT 5

16 GOLDEN MEADOW MAN FOUND DEAD IN BAYOU he was 33 years old.
Local Fighter "Indian Outlaw"
March 19, 2011 — Houma Today
www.houmatoday.com/story/news/2011/03/19/one-dead-after-boat-sinks-in-golden-meadow/26966676007/

17 *Chur*: Cajun slang for buttocks

18 ***Smashing Pumpkins***
A popular alternative rock band of the 1990s. Their song Today plays during Ramey's chaotic experience at Possumpalooza.

THE INDIAN OUTLAW

19 ***Forrest Gump***
The titular character of the iconic 1994 film, known for his simple wisdom and memorable quotes. Ramey channels Lieutenant Dan during a stormy boat ride.

BAR BRAWLERS AND SHOT CALLERS

20 "**Closing Time**" was written by Dan Wilson, the lead singer of Semisonic. **March 1998** as the lead single from their album *feeling Strangely fine*. The song became an anthem of endings—bars, relationships, and chapters—

MIDNIGHT MERCY

21 A **DWI (Driving While Intoxicated)** means a person was operating a vehicle while their ability to drive was impaired by alcohol or drugs. It's a legal charge that says the driver's judgment, reaction time, or coordination was affected enough to make driving unsafe. Laws vary by state, but a DWI usually involves arrest, fines, license restrictions, and court requirements because it's considered a serious public-safety risk.

About the Author

R.B. Rouge writes like she's outrunning a curse and testifying at the same time. Her stories bleed Southern shadows — stitched from secrets, scars, and the kind of family you survive by storytelling.

This ain't a healing circle. It's a holy reckoning. Misfitted, and mouthy, she names what others won't and calls it fiction so it makes it past the gatekeepers.

She writes for the bloodline-bound, the code-breakers, and the ones who hear static in their dreams.

Because the truth?

Still costs too damn much.

You can connect with me on:

- https://rb-rouge.com
- https://x.com/r3rouge
- https://facebook.com/r3rouge

Also by R.B. Rouge

R.B. Rouge is a published author and artist with two decades of work behind her, and a retired hairdresser raised deep in the South Louisiana bayou. Her storytelling walks the line between fact and fiction, stitching trauma with wit and memory with myth. With roots scorched by generational pain and stories that refuse to stay buried, she writes for those born into the fire—those who carry the scars and still choose to leave something better behind.

Born to fail (2005)
Intentionally buried. Never reprinted. Out of print. five stars. Buried on purpose. But some stories don't stay dead. ***They wait.***

Healed Expressions
PTSD Drawing Journal for Woman
By: RB Rouge

www.ingramcontent.com/pod-product-compliance
Ingram Content Group UK Ltd.
Pitfield, Milton Keynes, MK11 3LW, UK
UKHW021907190726
13853UKWH00002B/557